Equilibrium

A Novel

by

S. L. Watson

Equilibrium by S.L.Watson.

ISBN   978 1 7384454 0 0

First Edition 2024 Published by 'Prioda Publishing'

Printed in Glasgow in 2024 by McCormick Print
and Promotion, 15 Hillcrest Drive, Newton Mearns,
Glasgow G77 5HH

*"Your head is full of broken bottles which jag
your brain every now and again."*

Thomas Watson: my father, circa 1975

Stuart Watson was born in 1962 and grew up in Drumchapel,
Glasgow, a post war housing estate located in the north west of
the city.

This is his first novel.

*This book is dedicated to my wife Karen,
for her encouragement and support and to whom
I promised she would see in print before Cancer
takes her away from me.*

Chapter 1

It was mid-July in the hotter than usual summer of 2018 and as the noon deadline approached in Quito, capital city of Ecuador located at the northern tip of the Andes in South America, Antonio Varas, President and leader of the *Nueva Herencia* party was experiencing a mix of emotions.

If the video conference he was about to participate in went according to plan, he stood to gain politically, financially and most importantly, reputationally. He knew well that with all three, his political power would be consolidated, which in turn would enable him to continue to shape his homeland in line with his long held personal vision of the future.

It was a fact that Varas had a mandate from all five branches of his government to proceed with the audacious plan that he had recently outlined to them, a plan in which he had furiously championed over the previous month since it was first proposed to the Ecuadorian parliament. The only issue he could foresee as a real problem would be the drug cartels, whose existence he could not tolerate nor control, and who would undoubtedly look to exploit his plans for their own gains.

His marble walled office was one of the finest in the city and although the air conditioning was working efficiently, keeping the room temperature at a cool 65 degrees, he was nonetheless sweating profusely. There were just eight months left of his allotted time in office and despite his radical reform plan and best ethical efforts, he was in real danger of losing the next Presidential election to Sanchez Esperanza's *Magenta* Party, his closest political rivals whose manifesto reeked of hollow promises, personal greed and corruption.

If he could just close this much agonised over deal, the economic benefits to the country would be enormous, and the resulting increase in jobs and infrastructure would be the most significant economic boost to the relatively poor nation in its entire history. That however he pondered, would be nothing compared to the anticipated stratospheric increase in international investment, which would likely bring unprecedented wealth, prosperity and much needed American dollars to the nation's economy for at least the next thirty years.

Not only would this arrangement sway the undecided electorate, ensuring Varas the political victory he craved and a further four-year term in office to achieve his goals, it would also secure his legacy to the land, that for all of his forty-four years, he was proud to call home.

Plagued by child poverty for over 120 years, and desperately falling far short of the standards of their North American neighbours and allies in the west, Ecuador's lack of a compulsory education system for children, had a significant bearing on why the whole country was trailing so far behind many of the world's leading economies.

The lack of an adequate education system was a major factor directly responsible for the dependency of families on child labour which, aided by the attraction of easy money on offer by the drug cartels, were for most families the only viable sources of financial income, perpetuating the downward spiral of social depravation, poverty and violence.

Just over three years ago, Varas had been elected on his promise to break this cycle, and although he had begun well and made some progress, he was still far short of the goals that his personal vision had aspired to. Yes, it was true. He had to make concessions in a bid to secure this important deal that would help achieve his ambition and secure his future as President, but that was business and as far as he was concerned, it was a win-

win situation for Ecuador, a situation which left his conscience as clean as white linen.

It was a little under one month previously, in June 2018, while at a trade conference in Geneva where Varas 'by chance' was introduced to Max Simpson, an executive of *Bectel Incorporated*, a worldwide global conglomerate and major world player in the construction, shipping and telecommunications sectors, who were responsible for key infrastructure development projects in progress all around the globe.

Having engaged Varas in conversation, Simpson had intimated that, among their many other ventures, his organisation was interested in developing various philanthropic projects around the world. He went on to allude that Bectel's research and development branch had identified Ecuador as a potential site for investment which fitted the ethical parameters of Bectel's humanitarian aid profile, and was a worthwhile cause in which his company were willing to support. Like a seasoned hunter Max Simpson was baiting his trap and all of his instincts told him that his quarry had just caught the scent.

What on the surface appeared to Varas as a somewhat casual invitation to dinner that evening, at the Ritz-Carlton Hotel de la Paix in central Geneva where Max occupied the Penthouse Suite, was eagerly accepted. In actuality, nothing could have been further from the truth. The meeting and dinner invitation were carefully orchestrated plans resulting from many months of research and intelligence by members of Bectel's Intelligence and Security Division.

From his own standpoint and eager to explore any avenue that could perhaps cement his political future, President Antonio Varas from Ecuador had decided that little harm could come of hearing what the suave, impeccably dressed Englishman had to say and accepted the invitation wholeheartedly.

The intimate dinner that evening went on for over two hours and was a lavish affair, somewhat outwith Antonio's experience. Yes, he enjoyed the 'privileges of office' in his home country however, as was clearly demonstrated here and now, 'privilege' was a relative term. Promoting himself and his government as free from corruption, Varas was careful how he spent his city's finances and expensive Swiss hotels and fine wines were definitely not something he could justify to his electorate, especially when his country endured the shame of one of the world's worst child poverty ratings. Simpson however, aware of the ethical dilemma such an invite would pose for the President, made it quite clear from the outset that to avoid any domestic political issues the Ecuadorian Premiere was to be his honoured guest for the evening.

During the dinner Max spoke eloquently and with skill, keeping the main business until his guest was a trifle more relaxed. He touched on Golf and Tennis, which he knew were both passions of the South American, and spoke of classic European sports cars, which although not an owner, was a subject in which Antonio Varas was very well versed.

Almost as a lead as to where the conversation was going to end up, Max complemented Varas on his reputation of personal integrity whilst in office, alluding to the fact that he was familiar with the work *Nueva Herencia* had accomplished, despite many difficulties in its short three years and three months in office. Simpson was also sure to make the point that he was aware of the direction in which the Presidents vision was heading, subtly indicating that perhaps the Varas government's interests, and that of Bectel, could possibly be in alignment.

What Max Simpson did not disclose to his guest was that Bectel's top secret Intelligence and Security Division had been following his career for his entire term in office and had a dossier on him that was more than two inches thick. Simpson had done his homework and knew all about Varas. From his childhood in Quito, through his early teenage years when his elder sibling Manolo was killed aged 18, by a drug gang for whom he refused to deal drugs. He knew about Antonio's wife Emilia, and her charity work as First Lady that took up most of her time, and he knew about their four-year-old daughter Elena, and the calcium deficiency which was hampering her development. Most of all Simpson knew about Sebastian, a former tennis coach now Antonio's private secretary and secret lover. But there was no requirement to reveal this information. Not yet!

It was almost 10pm and the dinner, which was possibly one of the finest meals Varas had ever eaten, was over. The personal chef and four penthouse service staff that had been in attendance were thanked personally by Simpson and each handed a small envelope containing a substantial cash gratuity, in recognition of their excellent service. With the additional staff dismissed, the only two occupants of the suite were left with a bottle of Remy Martin's finest Louis XIII Baccarat cognac, which Varas later learned cost over $4,000 a bottle, complimented by a box of Cohiba Rubustos Cuban cigars, an equally expensive indulgence.

Although it was summertime in Geneva, the proximity to the Alps made the air cold and the log fire crackled welcomely as Varas and Simpson sat opposite each other on opulent matching red leather Chesterfield sofas, sipping and savouring the amber liquid, with nothing but a walnut coffee table and their respective ambitions separating the two. In different circumstances, Varas thought to himself, he would be sharing this scene with Sebastian however that was a part of his life that he was not prepared to discuss with the Englishman, or anyone else for that matter.

"So," Max began, blowing a satisfied cloud of cigar smoke over the top of his brandy glass. "Have you had enough to eat? Can I get you anything else? Please help yourself to more cognac."

nodding towards the crystal decanter which Simpson had strategically placed on a coaster next to the cigar box, both of which were conveniently within arm's reach of Varas.

"I am fine, thank you," said Antonio with a look of genuine gratitude on his face.

"Before this brandy takes effect, I would be interested to hear at what you hinted at earlier Max, 'various philanthropic projects' I think is what you said?"

"No time to lose," remarked Simpson. "You are quite right my dear fellow."

For the next forty minutes Max Simpson outlined how the company he represents were proposing to invest in, build and initially fund an entire education system in Ecuador, from pre-school right up to university level. Commencing as soon as national agreement could be reached, the city of Quito was to be the starting point, thereafter spreading to the rest of the nation. Once this project had achieved success, Simpson pointed out, other worldwide investors would no doubt follow suit, lining up to add their names, reputations, and most importantly their dollars, to Ecuador's salvation.

"Bectel," Max continued, "under your government party's leadership, are proposing an initial cash injection of five billion U.S. Dollars, with more to follow to a maximum of 15 billion over the next three years as the project develops."

"This would not only kick start your education initiative and bring much needed employment to the region in the short term, but properly managed this could mark the turnaround of your country's fortunes and bring the whole region out of poverty and onto the world stage."

"A worthy long-term vision, don't you agree Mr Varas?"

Varas sat in his chair motionless, suddenly conscious that his mouth was gaping wide open. Was this man reading his mind? Good job he had never become a poker player as with a 'tell' like that, he would have been bankrupt in a week.

Varas had not seriously considered success in re-election as a reality yet as he had been too busy getting his teeth into what needed done in the latter half of his first term in office, hoping this would be sufficient. This proposal, which was like a gift from heaven, would certainly change all that.

"Please go on Mr Simpson," he said with salivating anticipation in his voice. "You have kindled my imagination."

"As an added incentive to work with us, a deal sweetener so to speak," Max continued "my employer is also willing to construct and finance a separate side project, for which we would require the approval of your Transport and Social Control committee," subtly indicating his knowledge of the intricacies of the Ecuadorian political system.

Ecuador's Transport and Social Committee, was a branch of the government responsible for Social Development and Infrastructure, which along with the Executive, the Legislative, the Judicial and the Electoral, make up the five branches of the Ecuadorian government. The President leads the Executive branch which has oversight of all the other aspects of government business. Simpson was well aware of this and knew that, despite the pretence of democracy, the Executive Branch had the final say on all political decisions.

Simpson went on. "What Bectel are looking to accomplish is to design and build an international auditorium and concert venue in Ecuador, similar to the famed 'Hollywood Bowl' in the USA, only grander in scale and much more innovative in design," "and," he continued before Varas could form any questions, "the location we have identified for this structure is on the edge of the jungle, approximately 10 miles to the west of the city of Quito."

"This is a project for which my employer has a great passion Mr Varas, and I cannot stress how important it is to him that this auditorium gets the go ahead without interference in any way from your government."

Continuing with his forward momentum he added, "we would of course comply with all of your national building and labour regulations, and will draw most of the workforce from your city, offering your citizens an attractive salary in return."

"I am sure I do not have to spell out the tax revenue possibilities from this for your future government, Mr Varas."

Max Simpson also went on to outline the citywide supporting infrastructure Bectel were prepared to invest in, to make the entertainment venue work. He highlighted the economic benefits in terms of both short and long term employment, and the clever marketing strategy that would make this project one of the most desired and innovative entertainment venues in the world, attracting not only the biggest names in music and entertainment, but also the plethora of international citizens that would flock to the area to patronise such events.

Simpson made a particular point of underlining the projected spend, such so called 'entertainment junkies' would contribute to Ecuador's economy, on an ongoing and sustainable basis.

"Just so we are clear Mr Varas", he went on, "our educational aid project funding package for your country is conditional, that condition being that Bectel's auditorium project at Quito receives your immediate approval."

"Your government would, of course, be at liberty to spin this decision in any way they see fit however I must stress that this aspect of our proposal is NOT negotiable." Despite the friendly tone of his conversation throughout the entire evening, Max

Simpson's emphasis on the word *NOT* had a definitive air of authority about it which almost dared Antonio to deny him.

"I won't press you for a decision now Mr Varas, as obviously you must discuss this with your government." "My employer wants to move on this quickly therefore, with your consent, I will contact you for your decision in principle, at Mid-day Ecuadorian local time exactly thirty days from now and if we are in agreement, I can put my legal team on a contract for your signature and get started straight away."

To conclude his carefully orchestrated monologue, Max went on, "I would fully anticipate that your government will take all the credit for making this happen of course," he continued coming to the summary of the evening's events, "however it is imperative that you do not make any announcements to the media until we have a signed and binding contract. This is also a non-negotiable condition of our offer Mr Varas."

"I trust all of this is acceptable to you?" Max concluded, returning to the amicable persona he had adopted throughout the entire evening.

Presenting his dinner guest with an envelope, Max said, "Here you will find an outline of the proposal we have just been discussing which you may peruse at your leisure as I do realise old boy, I have given you quite a lot to think about," he said with a polite laugh.

"Please reflect carefully on what I have said Mr Varas. I won't be meeting you again in person however like I said, I will contact you in thirty days for your decision."

Returning to his authoritative tone he added, "Incidentally and a word to the wise, Mr Varas. If you cannot convince your government of the benefits of our proposal, my employer will seek another neighbouring President who can." This parting shot from Max Simpson had an air of finality about it and reminded the President that, despite the boost to his aspirations that this offer represented, he would do well to remember that firmly on the ground was where his feet belonged.

The Englishman ended the meeting with "I will now bid you goodnight and thank you for your most excellent company," Max said amicably, leading his guest into the hallway and gently closing the heavy contemporary oak door to his suite behind him.

A short time later, his Swiss security detail travelling in separate vehicles in front and behind, in standard three car convoy configuration, President Antonio Varas sat alone in the rear of his limousine on the ride back to his own hotel. Uncharacteristically he did not converse with his driver but instead was emersed deep in thought, his head spinning with the possibilities that could arise from the lengthy discussion which had just taken place.

The opulent surroundings of the Ritz-Carlton Hotel penthouse suite were but now a fading memory as Varas entered the chambers of his own modest but still luxurious accommodation, which was set slightly further back from the waterfront. As he approached his suite, he thanked the head of his security detail for their patience and professionalism, one of the few foreign dignitaries that took the trouble to do so, apologising for all the inconvenience he had no doubt caused them.

Lieutenant Andre Kaufmann of the Geneve Gendarmerie, the commander of that evening's security detail, was somewhat taken aback by the expression of humble gratitude, uncharacteristic behaviour for this type of world leader, and acknowledged President Varas's kind comments by clicking his heels together and bowing his head towards the man.

"Thank you, sir," he said. "I will pass on your kind and thoughtful comments to my team."

Kaufmann continued, "Of course sir, there will be officers posted outside your door throughout the night." "If you require anything of me or my colleagues, then please make your wishes known to us, and it shall be so."

The Lieutenant concluded with, "I will now bid you goodnight sir, and I hope you have an uneventful return to your country in the morning." adding "A relief security team will attend tomorrow at the appointed time to escort you to the airport." He ended the conversation with another click of his heels and disappeared into an adjacent room, where he and his team were settling in for the night.

Sebastian was waiting inside Varas's suite, dressed in a white bathrobe which accentuated the brownness of his tanned athletic legs. He had been watching television with his feet, cosseted in a pair of suede and sheepskin slippers, propped up on the coffee table and had a large glass of white wine in his hand. He looked over as the President entered the suite and as soon as he saw Antonio's ashen face, he knew something was amiss.

"Oh, my goodness Antonio," he said with genuine concern. "You look so pale. Is everything alright?"

Despite the several glasses of wine and the two large brandies he had consumed, Antonio felt remarkably unaffected by the alcohol. Perhaps it was the food in his belly acting as a sponge, perhaps the slow and steady pace of the dinner or was it the shock of what had just been offered to him on a plate, the latter of which was most likely to be the reason for his apparent sobriety. Or perhaps it was the ramifications for his dreams and aspirations that such an offer represented that was responsible for bringing his brain into focus. Was it shock or euphoria? At that precise moment Antonio really could not tell.

As his boss and friend relayed Max Simpsons words to the best of his recollection, Sebastian sat aghast, listening intently and asking for clarification at various points, as Antonio recited the chronology of the evening's events.

"Are you sure about this?" Sebastian asked in disbelief.

"It's all in here," replied Antonio, wafting the envelope which Max had given him, not thirty minutes before.

"You know what this means Antonio?" Sebastian said, picking up on the tempo of Antonio's subdued excitement.

"Yes, my friend." "Yes, I believe I do."

Chapter 2

Back in the present time it was Friday 20 July 2018 and as the minutes counted down towards mid-day, and the landmark video conference with Bectel's deputy CEO Max Simpson, Antonio's mind was racing ahead.

He had alerted the local media that the government wished to make a statement, and to that end had arranged a press conference for 2.00pm that very afternoon, where carefully controlled 'leaks' hinted that there was a big announcement about to be forthcoming. He dared not allude to what that announcement would consist of, and left it to the rumour machine to come up with their own theories of what the government were planning. Soon all would become clear, he thought to himself.

Varas of course, had the full backing of his five branches of government who after much discussion unanimously voted in favour of the funding arrangement for the landmark education programme, primarily because it supported their governments manifesto pledges and was the right thing to do, but also because it meant a high probability of re-election, and a guarantee of their own job security for possibly the next four to eight years. The condition of the proposal that included the development of the entertainment auditorium was, as far as they were concerned, the cherry on the cake and it mattered not to Ecuador whether this entertainment venue was a roaring success or a resounding failure. The general consensus of opinion was that the education reform proposal alone was a worthwhile project that would write *Nueva Herencia* into the history books.

At exactly 12.00pm local time, the video screen sprang into life, with a high pitched electronic ring and the Bectel logo flashing up on the screen. The Bectel logo was a white globe, tilted to represent the Earth's 23.5 degree incline from the vertical, and radiating white lines from Pole to Pole, representing the lines of longitude crossed by lines of latitude, that are the cornerstones of global navigation. Completing the logo were the Words Bectel Inc, in bold red letters below the emblem.

Varas, his Vice President Miguel Hernandez and the head of the legislative branch Alfonso Ortega were the only three people in the room and, as the shrill ringtone tore them from their individual private thoughts, they exchanged glances. Uppermost in the minds of the three men was the thought that it had been already agreed by the executive team that, following successful completion of this video conference, Varas's government was hoping to get a news item out to its electorate in time for the weekend newspapers.

Varas took a deep breath and pressed the connect button on the control panel in front of him and immediately a high-definition image of Maxwell Simpson, deputy CEO of Bectel Inc, appeared on screen. Simpson was sitting at a contemporary modern desk constructed of what looked like a large slab of ivory coloured marble which was approximately 10cm thick and about three metres wide. The desktop was supported by two dark brown similarly thick pieces of marble, located about 75cm in from each end, effectively acting as the legs of the desk. This created a large gap in the centre of the piece, which is where Simpson sat on a dark brown executive leather chair, with his hands clasped just beneath his chin and his elbows shoulder width apart, resting on the table.

He was dressed in a green Harris Tweed jacket over a striped green shirt, dark coloured trousers and black brogue shoes, which disappeared down towards the marble floor at the bottom of the screen. Simpson was in his office in Villeneuve, at the eastern end of Lac Leman in Switzerland. He was sitting with his back to a glass wall which gave the impression that his office was open to the elements, through which there was a fantastic vista of Monte Rosa, Switzerland's highest peak, located in the snow-capped, Pennine Alps.

Max Simpson opened the conversation.

"Good afternoon, Mr President, gentlemen," he said with the authority of a man who already knew the answers to the questions he was about to ask.

"I would like to congratulate you and your team for your punctuality in this instance and thank you for considering the offer that Bectel had put before you last month."

"Tardiness in business is something that I quite simply cannot abide and it tells one a lot about an individual, don't you think?" Simpson added. On behalf of his team, Varas nodded politely without speaking. This faux expression of modesty was for the benefit of the South Americans. Simpson was already confident of what the outcome of the meeting would be, and plans were already in place that supported his prediction of the result.

"Please allow me to make some introductions." Simpson said, and in doing so pressed a button on a small console sitting on the tabletop in front of him, causing the camera to zoom out revealing two other people sitting at opposite ends of his desk.

"On my left here is Miss Natalie Caldwell, Director of our foreign affairs division."

Natalie Caldwell was 5 foot, 9 inches tall, blonde and of Scandinavian descent with piercing green eyes. A former Olympic swimmer she had achieved her position in the company through sheer talent. She was a Doctor of Law, had a master's degree (Hons) in world economics, a master's (Hons) in foreign affairs and a boasted a handicap of 5 on the golf course. At 34 years of age, she had an athletic figure which turned heads wherever she went. To this end, and to avoid unwanted attention, she dressed down most of the time and today had her hair pinned up, complimented by a tailored, dark two-piece Prada business suit with trousers, a plain white blouse with a mandarin collar and black patented court shoes with a four-inch stiletto heels. She was sitting in a similar executive chair to Simson but at the extremity of his desk, her hand resting on a pad on which she was taking notes. She looked up and raised her left hand in greeting.

"Good afternoon, gentlemen," she said. "I am very pleased to make your acquaintance."

"And on my right, may I introduce Mr Mathew Barnes-Smith." Simpson continued. "Mathew is Director of our legal division and has been instrumental in putting this proposal into a format that we hope you will find acceptable," again paying lip service to the trio on the other end of the camera. Barnes-Smith also raised a hand in acknowledgment of the Ecuadorians. Like his counterpart at the opposite end of the desk, Barnes-Smith was an expert in his chosen discipline. Impeccably dressed in a grey business suit complimented by a white shirt and blue silk tie, he was 50 years of age and a graduate of Harvard Law school. He was also a Doctor of Philosophy and had been a corporate lawyer for some of the biggest companies on the planet, before being 'headhunted' by Bectel.

Now fifteen years in post, Barnes-Smith was the architect of Bectel's operating parameters, and knew more than most about how to conduct effective business in every part of the world. It was Barnes-Smith who had had personally drafted the contract which would ratify the proposal between Bectel Inc and the Varas's government, a contract which at that very moment was sitting in a secure briefcase in the hands of a courier from Bectel's Intelligence and Security Division.

Sipping from a bottle of water in the entrance lobby of the

'Presidential Palacio de Carondelet', the very building where five floors above, the three South Americans were about to agree on the deal that would consolidate their political careers, the Bectel courier patiently awaited his summons.

"Good evening to you and your staff Mr Simpson." Varas began, trying to show that he was aware of the time differential, and that early evening had already begun in Switzerland.

"May I introduce you to Senior Miguel Hernandez, my Vice President," indicating the man to his left, "and Senior Alfonso Ortega, head of our legislative branch," motioning to the man sitting to his right. All three were dressed in unremarkable dark business suits and light coloured shirts, however only the President was wearing a tie. The men exchanged a few polite pleasantries about the weather in their respective parts of the world before getting down to business.

"So," Max began, still sitting with his elbows on the desk but now his hands were open and he was pressing his fingertips together. Looking straight into the camera he continued.

"Have you thought about our proposal, and do you have an answer for me, Mr Varas?" As he finished his sentence, he kept his hands together as if praying but pointed them directly at the camera and by implication, directly at the President.

Antonio cleared his throat and adopting a formal tone began.

"Mr Simpson. I speak with the full authority of the Ecuadorian government who, after careful consideration, have given me their unanimous support and their permission to accept your proposal and all of the terms attached thereto, specifically the development of your entertainment venue just outside Quito."

"That is splendid news Mr. President," said Simpson feigning his surprised delight. "Bectel are looking forward to working with you and I am confident we will both achieve our mutual goals from this new partnership."

Simpson continued, "May I ask Mr Varas that before we carry on, you place a call to your reception desk and ask that a Mr Bauer be brought to your office to join this meeting?"

"Mr Bauer," he added, anticipating the question, "is an employee of Bectel and is currently waiting in the reception lobby of your building. He has in his possession a final draft of the contract, identical to that those we have been working on, for signature from you and your colleagues. When I have this, we can proceed."

Varas did as requested and a few minutes later Jurgen Bauer entered the room. He was dressed in a business suit and carried an aluminium briefcase, which was chained to his left wrist. In front of the camera, Bauer unchained the briefcase and entered the combination to open it up, removing two large buff coloured folders, each with a copy of a completed business contract inside. This contract was a final draft of the Bectel proposal and was the product of several amended versions, as was common in many business arrangements. Varas and his team had already had sight of an electronic copy of the final document prior to today's meeting and were comfortable with the content and the wording. Still in view of the camera, and under the watchful eye of his boss over nine and a half thousand kilometres away, Bauer placed the folders on the desk in front of the President. Varas passed the folders to Ortega who opened the documents and after a brief scan, nodded his approval.

"If all three of you could kindly place your signatures on one of the copies where indicated Mr President," Simpson requested politely, "and pass the document to my colleague." "The second folder is your own copy. You will observe that both sets of documents already bear my signature."

The three South American Politicians did as requested, with

Varas signing the document last. Blowing the ink dry on the contract, Varas handed it to Bauer, who confirmed the signatures with a nod of his head towards the camera.

"Splendid Mr President," Simpson said with a smile. "So now to work." He turned to his right, addressing Barnes -Smith.

"Mathew, if you please."

Barnes-Smith took a mobile telephone from the breast pocket of his jacket and pressed some buttons. He said something in French to the person on the other end of the phone and concluded with "Merci." He turned to his boss and with no hint of stress or emotion in his demeanour said, "It is done."

"Splendid. Thank you, Mathew," Simpson replied.

Dispassionately Simpson turned, and staring directly into the camera continued.

"Mr President. Five billion US dollars have just been transferred to the Ecuadorian government account you had previously specified to us, and you may begin to promote your educational reform programme." "You will receive a further five billion, exactly one year from today and the balance of five billion the following year, as per our agreement."

"You are now free to publicise the agreement between Bectel and your government in any way you see fit, and in support of your own political ambitions."

"Also, for your information," Simpson again stated with arrogant certainty in his voice. "A large party of staff from Bectel will be landing at Mariscal Sucre International Airport in Quito, in just under six hours' time. They have been instructed to secure our construction site and begin operations to recruit staff to assist with our project, on which we intend to break ground in no more than two months' time. Please have an official from your

Transport and Social Control branch meet them and afford them any assistance they require."

This statement from Simpson alluded to his confidence that the Bectel proposal would be accepted, as his team were already in the air prior to the deal being ratified, however Varas and his two colleagues failed to pick up on this rather obvious display of arrogance.

"Similarly," Simpson continued, "there will be several large ships arriving at your Puerto Bolivar docks over the next few weeks. I will ensure your government receives the details."

"These ships contain personnel and specialised equipment required for our project near to Quito." "Please make similar arrangements for a reception and assistance."

Varas responded as politely and diplomatically as he could, nodding his head in acknowledgement. "Ecuador thanks you and your company Mr Simpson, for what I hope will be a lasting and productive partnership."

"I will personally ensure your instructions are carried out to the letter."

"I appreciate that Mr President," Simpson replied.

"Finally, may I say that business from this end will be conducted from now on by Miss Caldwell, who will be your main point of contact." "I intend to focus on other aspects of our global operations however I will retain oversight of our mutual progress."

"If there is nothing else, then I will leave you to prepare for your press announcement and I wish you and your government, every success in your education reform programme and forthcoming election."

"Mr Bauer," Simpson added, addressing the courier who was still in the room.

"Yes sir?" the man responded.

"A company jet is on the tarmac at Mariscal Sucre Airport awaiting your attendance. Kindly board this aircraft with due expedience and deliver the contents of your attaché case directly to Miss Caldwell."

"Yes sir." Bauer nodded his compliance and left the room as Max Simpson ended the call with a press of a button.

Antonio Varas made two calls immediately following the conclusion of the meeting. The first was to confirm that the government coffers had in fact received a cash transfer of five billion US Dollars, and the second was to his contacts at the local TV and press offices, confirming a government press conference at 2.00pm that day where a major announcement on education would be forthcoming.

Max Simpson made just one call following the meeting. That call was directly to Harrison Becker CEO and Head of Bectel Inc, on his very private, very secure line.

With impassive efficiency he simply said to the recipient, "Sir, the initial phase of operation *Black Horse* is complete, and on schedule."

"Thank you, Max." came the reply. "Delegate and move on."

Chapter 3

The *Democratic Republic of the Congo,* also known as the DRC, is located in central Africa and is the second largest country on the African continent, with a current population of around 105 million people. Since the end of the 19th Century until recently the country has known nothing but turmoil and conflict.

In the Colonial years, when the more developed northern European nations were scrambling to divide up Africa, the country was 'acquired' by King Leopold of Belgium who in 1885 claimed the region as his own personal property and with the aid of his colonial military unit, known as the *Force Publique*, coerced the indigenous population into producing rubber for export to affluent Europe and the Americas. Those of the population who did not perish due to the consequences of exploitation and slave labour, died of disease which was rampant at that time as a result of the appalling conditions the population had to endure. In 1908 King Leopold reluctantly ceded the land to the government of Belgium who declared the area be renamed as the '*Belgian Congo*'.

Although known by a different title, the relentless exploitation of the region, its resources and its people continued, up until 1960 when on the 30th June of that year, the country gained independence from Belgium and declared itself '*The Republic of the Congo*'.

Instability and poverty, the breeding grounds for rebellion, as ever were never far away during this period and in 1971 following a *coup d'état* the country was renamed '*Zaire*', and became a one-party Dictatorial State, with corruption rife in government and internal tribal conflict doing little to promote any form of economic stability.

In 1994 Mass genocide in neighbouring Rwanda again destabilised the region, which became the trigger for the Rwandan Militia led, invasion of Zaire which occurred just two years later. As a consequence of this invasion in late 1996, the country's name was again changed by the incoming President Laurent-Desire Kabila to the *'Democratic Republic of the Congo'*, a title which remains to the present day. In the five-year war that raged between 1998 to 2003, the country was devasted by a conflict which involved nine other nations and in excess of twenty, armed militia groups, all fighting for supremacy and the promotion of their own religions and ideals.

The democratic election of 2018 resulted in the appointment of Hinshi Womboto, the charismatic leader of the *Mayola Party* as the country's new leader, where democracy would be seen to prevail and where the first ever peaceful transition of power in the country's entire history would occur.

Womboto, who was born in Kinshasa the country's capital, was a 48 year old moderate, who's vision promised positive change for the country. Educated at Cambridge university in the UK, he gained a Master's degree in international politics and a BA in business administration, as well as rubbing shoulders with a myriad of people who were soon to be in positions of power and influence in the northern European nations. Womboto quickly realised that to succeed, he would need to unify all of the opposing factions who were scrambling for power in the DRC, his efforts successfully bringing calm and compromise to a region that had known little more than war, persecution, poverty and death.

President Womboto was elected principally on the strength of his message to the people of the DRC which was essentially that the country's colossal wealth, in terms of its natural resources, would be shared by all.

In practical terms, his message to the electorate was that peace and stability would be the catalysts that would stimulate the more advance nations to invest the expertise and colossal financial reserves required to make the extraction of these natural resources economically viable. He concluded his message with the statement that political stability, which was what his party was promising, would be the engine that would deliver prosperity to all.

As the DRC was a long-standing member of the United Nations, Womboto naturally attended UN council meetings and at his first conference as the country's leader, in New York in September 2018, he reminded the world of the suffering that the people of his country had endured for more than 100 years. Womboto outlined his vision of the future for a democratic, prosperous and stable nation and appealed for the wealthiest members of the UN to assist, which coincidentally is exactly what the UN council wanted to hear.

"My first priority," he said with genuine sincerity, "will be the welfare of our people, and it is my true belief that a healthy and aspirational population, will be the driving force behind our future prosperity."

"To this end," he continued, "I have already concluded talks with an investor who is willing to speculate on the success of my government," putting much emphasis on the word *my*, "and I wish to announce to the council that a world leading hospital complex has already began construction in Kisangani, in the central north region of our country."

"This new development will be entirely self-sufficient, in terms of funding and energy, and will bring to central Africa the kind of cutting-edge medical expertise that has until now been the provision of only the wealthiest nations in the world." "Not only will this facility cater for the casualties of war, who are my long suffering brothers and sisters, but it will also be open to our neighbours, with whom for so many years we have been embroiled in conflict."

"I hope and I pray that these measures will be the first steps towards healing the physical wounds of the past and ensure that the people of the DRC, and all of her neighbours in the Sub-Saharan region, are fit and ready to pursue the labours that will bring about their rightful destiny."

He concluded his speech to rapturous applause and much 'back patting' and shaking of hands. Womboto retook his seat in the sure knowledge that the world news media would be focusing on the DRC for weeks to come, with his name being closely aligned with the country's anticipated success.

Although not yet in the public domain, Womboto's vision was being realised with the expertise and huge financial resources of Bectel Inc. Sensing Womboto's rise to power in 2017, Bectel had begun secret negotiations on an aid package to deliver the hospital facility that would have the physical impact, the technical and medical expertise and the funding to deliver what Womboto would later promise in his speech to the UN council.

The deal with Bectel, in essence, represented the political capital that Womboto would rely on as a mechanism that would significantly increase the likelihood of foreign investment in the area and make the DRC the talking point of the global community, but this time for all the right reasons.

The deal, which Womboto would later speak of, was secretly codenamed *RED HORSE*, that codename being known only to a privileged few at Bectel, one of whom was Max Simpson. The organisation's second in command had been in covert negotiations with Hinshi Womboto since Bectel's Intelligence and Security Division had indicated his popularity was on the ascent, one year previously.

Believing the old adage that 'there is no such thing as a free lunch', Womboto naturally suspected that Bectel would be looking for something tangible in return for their considerable financial investment.

Propagating this plausible arrangement, Max Simpson persuaded Womboto that Bectel was indeed expecting to be granted future access to the seams of Platinum rich ore that 'cris crossed' the subterranean landscape of his country. Such a licence to extract this ore, reasoned Womboto, would bring significant economic income, and provide much needed employment in the region.

At the negotiation stage of the deal, addressing Womboto, Max Simpson had previously said;

"My employer is prepared to be patient with his plans to extract and process the Platinum ore from your country Mr Womboto." Simpson explained, adopting a tone that could only convey the illusion that he was prepared to compromise to get what he wanted. "And we do so in order that it does not appear that you are being," he paused momentarily, "influenced in your vision, by any third party."

The reality of the situation was that nothing could have been further from the truth. Simpson was ruthless in pursuit of Bectel's objectives and nothing would prevent him from achieving those. If Womboto could not be persuaded with 'honey', he pondered, then he would be eliminated and replaced by someone else with a 'sweeter tooth'. After all, Simpson mused to himself. If the previous President had been a little more ambitious, he wouldn't be having this conversation with Womboto now.

On the face of it, Max Simpsons proposal to delay Bectel's

Platinum extraction goals until three years into Womboto's successful election term, made sense and suited both parties. For Womboto, it would show the world that the DRC was not a puppet government, prepared to 'jump into bed' with anyone who offered a financial handout, thereby boosting his credibility as a leader competent enough to tread the boards on the world stage. For Bectel however it negated the need to devote huge financial resources to a cover story that was never intended to come to fruition.

It was now January 2020, and at the hospital construction site approximately 15km west of Kisangani in the north of the country, serviced by nearby Bangoka Airport and easily accessed from the nearby N3 national highway, things were going according to plan. The fabric of the main hospital and associated buildings had begun to rise out of the parched landscape and indications were that, as promised, this would be a world beating facility.

At over 300 metres in length, the main structure looked like a gigantic 'Celtic cross' from the air, with protrusions that pointed north to south and east to west. Located at the central part of the cross was a large circular construction which, when completed, would eventually be six stories high and be the main administrative area of the building where the labs, offices, refectories and operating theatres would be located. This central structure was itself more than one hundred metres in diameter. The span of the cross that went from west to east, was shorter than its neighbouring axis at just 200 metres.

Impressive as it was, the main hospital building did not generate as much interest or controversy as the *On Site Independent Power Station* (*OSIPS*), being built nearby. Located a half km to the west of the main project, the power station was an architectural enigma. With a nod to the ancient Egyptian engineers who designed and constructed the Great Pyramids, over two thousand years previously, the *OSIPS* structure was a gargantuan, three-sided pyramid.

The pyramid stood a massive 200m from base to vertex, over 60m taller than the great pyramid of Giza, with each of its three baseline edges being 200m in length. like the Great Pyramids in Egypt, it was a marvel of engineering for its time however the innovation on this particular structure was on the inside and was unlikely to be seen by anyone, save those involved in the construction.

The structure was set in such a manner that one of the edges of the base was perpendicular to the cardinal compass point west. This had the effect, when viewed from above, of making the OSIPS look like a gigantic 'play button' on the landscape, attracting it the local nickname, the *'Play Station'*. The power source for the 'Play Station' remained a closely guarded secret, known only to the chief engineers and architects of Bectel, and at present remained the only outstanding element of the structure.

Known only to a few key individuals, inside the *OSIPS* at ground level and invisible to prying eyes were 77 metal cylinders, each constructed of 100mm thick steel alloy, each 9.5metres in diameter and 40 metres in depth. these cylinders were sunk into the earth so that their tops were at ground level, and were arranged to comply with the internal baseline of the structure, looking somewhat similar to the red balls in the frame used to set up a snooker table.

Each individual cylinder was linked to two others at its base, 40m below ground level, by a network of circular ducts just 60cm in diameter. these connection ducts would facilitate the mixture that would eventually be poured into the cylinders, achieve a uniform level. The spaces between each cylinder were back filled with soil originally excavated from the site leaving what was essentially, 77 tubular holes in the ground.

Chapter 4

May 2020

Although the 'Play Station' pyramid at Kisangani was in essence a completed structure, the remainder of the hospital complex, like many other projects throughout the world, was on hold due the COVID 19 Pandemic that was sweeping the globe.

As the weeks rolled on to mid-summer of 2020, most of the Northern European nations found themselves on lockdown in an attempt to contain the spread of the Coronavirus. Sub-Saharan Africa was in a similar position to Northern Europe but, due to under reporting and manipulation of the figures, it seemed to the world that the pandemic had not yet affected the region to the same extent.

This situation, although not of their doing, allowed some flexibility as regards the movement of goods and people in the region and Bectel intended to take full advantage of it to finalise the construction of their power plant ready, or so it would seem, for when the crisis would abate and construction of the hospital complex could resume.

In reality, the delay in full lockdown permitted the so called 'Play Station' to be finalised for its true and deadly purpose, that purpose being known only to relatively few individuals, all of whom were in the employment of Harrison Becker, CEO of Bectel Inc.

In the month of August 2020, whilst the rest of the world struggled to combat the ongoing pandemic, each of the 77 cylinders within the pyramid at Kisangani had been injected almost to the brim, with what many believed to be some form of liquid concrete, topped with a 100mm layer of magnesium chippings. The bulk of the material in each cylinder, the composition of which was a closely guarded secret, was produced at Bectel's chemical refinery in Rotterdam and shipped by ocean going tanker to the Port of Matadi, which sits on the Congo River in the extreme west of the DRC. From Matadi, the product was transported overland by rail to the construction site at Kisangani, in what seemed to be and endless procession of rail freight tankers each capable of holding 130,000 litres of the mixture.

By late September the 'Play Station' was now fully complete, having received almost 242,000 cubic metres of the product, which to the layman resembled brown sludge. Because of the substance's appearance, and the fact that concrete was a feature of many nuclear reactors around the world, speculation led to the belief that some sort of nuclear material would be involved in the production of the energy that was intended to fuel the hospital complex, and the natural conclusion to that rumour, was that the nuclear component would be transported to the site at the last possible moment.

On 28th September 2020, Harrison Becker was on board his private yacht, 34km off the coast of Portugal, where the sun was setting over the western horizon, when he received an encrypted call on his satellite telephone.

"Mr Becker?" The voice was that of Max Simpson, and it spoke with a timbre that exuded confidence.

"Yes Max," the head of Bectel replied.

"I am pleased to report sir that operation *RED HORSE* is now fully complete and primed."

"Thank you, Max," Becker replied. "Were there any issues?"

"Yes sir." "Unfortunately, there was a breach of our security policy, minor in nature, with one of the government officials who had questioned the construction parameters of the *RED HORSE* pyramid."

"The problem," Simpson chose his words carefully, "was *resolved* locally, without any further issues developing and the site is now in the hands of our Intel and Security Division."

"Splendid." was Becker's reply.

"And our other operations?" he enquired.

"All are proceeding according to schedule sir," Max reported efficiently, "and all three additional sites will be fully operational and ready in time for your chosen deadline."

"I expected nothing less Max," Harrison Becker replied, his voice brimming with self satisfaction.

"Thank you, sir," Max said with a soft voice, as his superior terminated the call.

The government official that Max Simson had alluded to during his call was Benjamin Ngoy, a specialist in the employ of Hermus Safi, the Minister for National Development.

Safi found his way into government office partly because he could articulate himself very well, partly because he mixed with the right influential people but principally because he was the incumbent president, Hinshi Womboto's first cousin.

At 55 years of age and officially designated Safi's aid, Ngoy was himself a qualified and highly experienced Architect with a background in civil engineering.

Prior to his call to serve in Womboto's government advising Safi, Ngoy had spent time on some of the biggest construction projects in the world including the San Roque Dam in the Philippines in

2003, and the Three Gorges Dam in China in 2008. Ngoy was considered an expert in all forms of construction that involved reinforced concrete, and enjoyed worldwide repute for his attention to detail.

The professional curiosity that was his signature trait however was about to result in the premature termination of his life.

It was around 4.30pm on a sunny Thursday afternoon, on the 24th September 2020, in the DRC capital Kinshasa, and the working day was coming to an end for most of the city's employees, but not for Benjamin Ngoy.

His boss, the Minister for National Development Hermus Safi, had decreed that a project of the significance of the central hospital construction project at Kisangani required extra effort and although there was no official mandate to do so, Safi expected his top executives, of whom Ngoy was the most revered, to go that extra mile to get the job completed on time.

"After all," Safi was once heard to remark. "Lives, but more importantly political futures depended on it."

Sitting at the drawing board of his contemporary office in the late afternoon, in the bustling business district of Kinshasa Ngoy, smartly dressed in a business suit with his jacket hung neatly on coat hanger, was sipping on a cup of coffee from the Starbucks café down in the foyer of his office building. The beverage had been thoughtfully brought to him by his secretary.

Reviewing the schematics of the pyramid structure at Kisangani, he came across what appeared to be an anomaly in the blueprints.

Whilst checking the calculations on the *OSIPS* structure he noticed that whilst two of the exposed faces of the tetrahedron, the ones which faced north east and south east were constructed of five-metre-thick reinforced concrete, the exposed face that was orientated exactly due west appeared to be constructed of only half metre thick concrete and contained only ten percent of the reinforcement of its neighbouring sides.

"That is barely enough steel to keep the western face upright," he thought to himself.

Unable to conceive a valid constructional reason for this anomaly, Ngoy immediately suspected these details to be an administrative error, probably due to the translation of the original plans, or a mistake attributable to the tardiness of one of his draughtsmen. In any event, he intended to take the issue up with the project manager when he carried out a snap inspection visit to the site the following day.

Just to be double sure he buzzed the intercom to his secretary, who had a small office just down the hall.

"Miss Mwepu," he said softly into the intercom.

"Yes sir?" came the reply.

"Before you finish for the day, could you please contact Bectel, at their global construction facility HQ in Switzerland, and request a copy of the construction plans for the pyramid they are building in Ecuador?" "I need to make some comparisons between that structure and ours, in order to check some calculations, I am running."

"I know they probably have already finished for the day," he continued, aware that Switzerland shared the same time zone as Kinshasa, "and I appreciate you are on your way out of the door yourself, so an e mail will suffice."

"That will give them tomorrow," he was referring to Friday, being the end of the working week, "to fulfil my request and get the plans sent over."

"I want to work on it this over the coming weekend," suddenly raising the timbre of his voice stating, "and where are my flight tickets to Kisangani?" he added as a noticeable afterthought, feigning frustration at his secretary's apparent lack of efficiency.

"Consider it done sir," she replied referring to the e mail request, with a hint of playful seduction in her voice.

Continuing, she went on. "Your flight leaves at 7.00am tomorrow morning sir, and there will be a rental car waiting for you at the other end. As you had intimated you were going to be late back tomorrow, and as the last flight out of Kisangani is around 5.00pm, I have taken the liberty of chartering a light aircraft for your return to Kinshasa, departing Kisangani at 9.00pm tomorrow night."

She ended her oration with, "And the flight tickets, car rental voucher and your travel itinerary are in the large envelope in your top desk drawer."

"Thank you miss Mwepu." "Extremely effectual as always," he concluded in a tone that confirmed his rebuke of a moment earlier was nothing more than a charade.

"Have a nice weekend and I will see you on Monday."

"Thank you, sir," she beamed. "Same to you."

Ngoy's secretary was Carmel Mwepu, a 24 year old native of Kinshasa. She was single and the oldest of three children, all girls, and was a tremendous source of pride to her parents with whom she still lived in the Kinshasa suburbs.

Commensurate with her employment aspirations, she had secured an important job with the government, which brought with it an attractive salary which in turn contributed to her family's comfortable lifestyle.

By all accounts Carmel was considered by many to be physically attractive but more importantly to her, she was a role model for her two younger siblings, Aline who was 16 and Pricilla who was 14, both of whom had aspirations to go to university.

Although not currently in a serious relationship, Carmel had dated a few men in her age group and older. It hadn't taken her long to learn how to manipulate the opposite sex with her smouldering good looks and athletic figure. She had no plans to marry in the short term and was busy building a financially secure future for herself, working at the government offices where she had a reputation for competence and efficiency.

At 55, her boss Ngoy was married but had no children of his own. Although he was old enough to be Carmel's Father, she had him wrapped around her little finger. Two years his personal assistant now, Carmel would flirt harmlessly with her boss as she frequently wandered in and out of his office on a daily basis. She could often feel his eyes burning into the back of her body, as she swayed her sylph like figure whenever she walked away from his desk. Ngoy, for his part would participate in the harmless charade, however there was an unspoken and definite 'line in the sand' between the two and evocative body language and genuine affection for the woman was as far as it went.

Ngoy kept Carmel employed because she was good at her job, and he viewed her with the protectiveness of a doting father. He had resolved two years earlier, shortly after taking her on, that fond of her as he was, he would do nothing to jeopardise their harmonious and mutually respectful, working relationship.

Chapter 5

Friday 25 Sept 2020

The following morning, the two-hour scheduled flight to Kisangani went without incident, and Benjamin Ngoy arrived refreshed at his destination. He had a coffee and a snack at the airport and then picked up his rented car, for the short journey to the hospital construction site.

Arriving at 10.30am Ngoy showed his pass at the main entrance to the site and was directed to the project office, which he had visited many times before in the previous two years. As he entered the office, he was immediately reminded of the gravity of his current appointment by the scale model of the hospital site and associated pyramid, which dominated the centre of the floor. The model was set on a table approximately 12 feet long and 6 feet wide, similar in size to a regulation snooker table and even at this scale, was truly impressive.

Despite his unannounced visit, Ngoy received an enthusiastic greeting.

"Benjamin!" exclaimed Christopher Green, Bectel's DRC Project Manager and company representative in charge of the whole site, breaking away from a discussion taking place at a drawing board at the far end of the room.

"It is so nice to see you again. How are you? How's the wife and all those cousins of yours?" he said, shaking Ngoy firmly by the hand.

"Hello Christopher, we are all fine thank you, and it is nice to see you again too," replied Ngoy politely.

The two men exchanged some other pleasantries, regarding their mutual acquaintances, and spoke briefly regarding the unusually hot weather they had been experiencing in recent months.

"Your timing is impeccable as I was planning on an early lunch." "Will you join me?" Green offered.

"I have already had something to eat thank you," replied Ngoy, "and have a light aircraft booked for my return journey, departing at 9.00pm. So, as I have a ton of work to get through on this visit, I will decline for the moment and just get straight to it."

"As you wish," replied Green.

"So, what brings you up this way then?" Green enquired, knowing full well the purpose behind Ngoy's surprise visit, a secret he was intent on keeping for the time being.

"Well," Benjamin began, "in addition to my usual progress and compliance visits to the site, I have some questions regarding the *OSIPS* blueprints." "Have you a moment, in private?"

"Of course," Green replied. "It's quite busy out here so why don't we go into my office and get away from the noise and the bustle."

Both men walked across the main floor and entered the project managers office. Just prior to closing the door Christopher Green called to his secretary sitting at her desk just outside.

"Samantha, hold all my calls please, and ensure I am not disturbed until further notice."

"Yes Mr Green," came the reply, as the door was purposefully closed.

"So, Benjamin," Green enquired seemingly surprised. "What's on your mind?"

"This!" said Ngoy, waving a metre long leather tube containing a set of plans in the air.

"May I?" Ngoy continued, motioning to Green's drawing board, which had a close schematic of the hospital's west wing currently displayed under a set of drawing aids. This aspect of the build is what Green was currently working on.

"Be my guest," replied Green, motioning to the drawing board with a smile.

Ngoy carefully extracted the blueprints for the *OSIPS* from his case and spread them out on the drawing board on top of what had previously been Green's current focus.

There were six sheets of plans in the leather tube, sheet 5 being the one that was uppermost in the stack and the subject of Benjamin Ngoy's current predicament.

Ngoy went on to explain the aspect of the *OSPIS* west face that was causing him concern. He intimated that, being constructed to the specifications these plans suggested, he doubted that the integrity of the west face would be able support itself let alone be able to withstand any geological activity, a phenomenon common in the area, without experiencing a catastrophic collapse.

Green stood beside him taking it all in. "You know this part of the project has already been completed and signed off to Bectel?" he said rhetorically.

"Yes," replied Ngoy. "That is why I am so concerned about this."

"I can assure you the *OSIPS* has been built to the highest standards," Green stated emphatically, "however I do acknowledge your concerns and I agree with your analysis."

"Construction to these parameters," he said, stabbing his finger onto the area of parchment that contained the dimensions of the west face of the pyramid, "would be a catastrophic miscalculation and almost certainly lead to a structural implosion." Expressing his initial analysis of the issue Green added, "This looks like a typo on the plans. That west face of the tetrahedron should be exactly the same as the two others."

"That's what I thought," exclaimed Ngoy, relieved that someone else agreed with his interpretation of these plans, which if correct was indeed a major cause for concern.

Green marched purposefully over to his office door, angrily yanking it open.

"Samantha." he bellowed from the doorway.

Samantha, Green's secretary who was not at her desk, was standing partway across the room collecting some letters from the printer when she heard the summons.

"Yes Mr Green?"

"Bring me the plans for the *OSIPS* immediately."

"Yes Mr Green," she replied, as she hurried over to the document safe located just behind her desk.

A few moments later Greens secretary entered the office with six sheets of blueprints for the *On Site Independent Power Station*, which as a local she knew as the 'Play Station', all rolled up and held together with rubber bands. She handed them to her boss and left the office, closing the door carefully behind her.

Green unravelled the plans and turned to page 5, the page in question, placing it on top of Ngoy's copy so the men could compare the two. The plans were identical in every detail except that Green's working copy indicated that the west face of the pyramid was constructed of five metre thick fully reinforced concrete, just like the other two faces.

Green let out a low whistle and exclaimed; "Thank goodness for that!"

"You really had me going there Benjamin. This must be a typing error made at your end. You really ought to have a word with that drawing team of yours and crack a few skulls. I don't know where you got your plans," Green said, forcing a light laugh, "but leave them for me to securely dispose of and I'll have Samantha prepare you a new *and correct* set in time for your flight home."

"Thank you, Christopher," replied Ngoy. "That is indeed a huge a relief to learn that."

"You are the only person I have spoken with regarding this, as no one else seems to have noticed. But if you don't mind, I will be holding on to these," Ngoy said, rolling his copy of the blueprints back into his leather case. "Someone's head is going to roll for this."

"No problem, Benjamin. As you wish."

"Now," and adopting a more relaxed and friendly tone Green said, "having taken this off your agenda, does that leave time for lunch?"

"Indeed, it does," replied Ngoy with a relieved smile, unaware that lunch with Christopher Green would be the last meal he would ever eat.

Ngoy could not possibly have known that earlier that morning, as Christopher Green had just stepped out of the shower in his hotel room in Kisangani, drying off his hair with a luxurious white towel, he received a call from Stanley Harding, Bectel's Director of Intelligence and Security. Harding had a reputation for ruthless efficiency and wielded the kind of power and wrath within the organisation that anyone who knew him, would not want to be the recipient of.

During the conversation Green was advised of Ngoy's request for duplicate plans regarding the pyramid in Ecuador, a request received the previous evening. Green was instructed to covertly ascertain what motivated Ngoy to make such a request.

"I believe he is coming to visit the site today," Harding remarked, reading from an intelligence brief he had been given just one hour previously, and speaking with the confidence that his intelligence was unchallengeable.

"As soon as you ascertain what he's up to, contact me directly." "As a precaution, I have already sent one of my special operatives to Kisangani." "He should be arriving late afternoon, today."

"He will not require anything from you except information, which he will get via my department, therefore it is vitally important that I am made aware of Ngoy's thoughts, intentions and movements, as soon as possible. Do I make myself clear on this Mr Green?" Green confirmed his understanding of the instruction and when the call was terminated, he sighed with relief and carried on with his preparations for the day.

Following the ad hoc lunch with Ngoy, both men were sipping coffee when Green excused himself to make an important call. In a quiet section of the restaurant, Green made a mobile call to Stanley Harding, relaying all the information he had discovered about Ngoy's findings regarding the *OSIPS* structure, and of his suspicions. Green advised that in his opinion, Ngoy was not buying the typo story and was insistent on seeing the structure for himself. Green was instructed by Harding that Ngoy was not to be permitted access to the *OSIPS* under any circumstances, and to delay his attendance there for as long as possible.

For the remainder of the afternoon Ngoy and Green inspected the main hospital complex, discussing the issues which the project faced and focusing on the progress that had been made, despite the ongoing worldwide pandemic and other logistical setbacks. Eventually Green could delay it longer and at about 7.30pm, and at Ngoy's insistence, they drove over to the *OSIPS,* which was a completed structure now in the hands of Bectel's Intelligence and Security Division.

"Can I help you gentlemen?" enquired a uniformed guard standing outside the security booth, at which there was a barrier adjacent to the only gap in the perimeter fence surrounding the structure. The guard was dressed in military camouflage which was black and grey in colour and was wearing a ballistic vest and a soft black cap on his head. Additionally, the guard was wearing an overt earpiece and microphone, that enabled him constant contact with his superiors. In his hand, supported by a strap around his shoulder he held a Heckler and Koch MP5 automatic machine gun, which was supplemented by a Glock 9mm pistol holstered on his right hip.

"Christopher Green, project manager and my guest, chief Architect, Benjamin Ngoy from the DRC government," Green barked efficiently at the officer. "We require access to the structure to check some construction details."

"May I see your identification passes please?" the guard replied dispassionately.

Green, who had been driving the site vehicle, handed both his and Ngoy's ID passes to the guard who took them over to the booth where one of his colleagues was sitting next to a computer terminal. A few moments later the guard returned and in the same dispassionate tone spoke with the men.

"Mr Green you may proceed within the perimeter fence however Mr Ngoy you may not, as it appears that your authorisation card has been revoked."

Ngoy looked at the guard, exasperated, and said; "But I have been to this site dozens of times in the last year." "There must be some mistake!"

Despite Ngoy's protestations, the guard would not budge and refused entry to the government officer.

"This is an outrage!" Ngoy protested, getting out of the vehicle to voice his displeasure and apply the weight of his government position, in an attempt to intimidate the man. Ngoy was a senior DRC government official and was not used to being denied anything, let alone being spoken to in such a manner by what he perceived to be nothing more than a 'trumped up' security guard.

As he walked round the car towards the man, the guard levelled his weapon and pointed it straight at Ngoy's chest. Both his demeanour and the stare of his cold dark eyes conveyed that he would have no hesitation in pulling the trigger and ending Ngoy's life, right there and then.

"Sir, I must insist that you to cease and desist and return to your vehicle," The guard ordered in the same flat tone, devoid of any emotion as before. "If you take one more step towards me, I will fire."

Ngoy stopped dead in his tracks, the road dust from his angry strides swirling in the air before settling in a thin film on his shoes. Not at all happy but convinced this man, a native African like himself, meant what he said, Ngoy retreated back to the relative safety of the vehicle, adamant that this guard had not seen the last of him.

Green returned to the main site office with Ngoy, who although very angry at what had just taken place, was visibly shaken by his ordeal. Despite attempts to calm him down, Green was unable to placate the government officer who gathered up his belongings and returned to his car, leaving the site for the airport where his light aircraft would be waiting to take him back to Kinshasa.

Chapter 6

It was 6.15pm earlier that same evening when a middle-aged man, with a distinguished aura surrounding him, knocked on the office door of the airport director at Kisangani. He was tall with a sallow complexion, a neatly manicured grey beard and grey hair, dressed in a dark double-breasted blazer and light-coloured slacks. The man's face had a texture about it which exuded the kind of wisdom that only comes from hardship and experience.

Producing a small leather wallet with a badge and an identity card, which would confirm what he was about to say, he introduced himself as Pierre Dubreton, a Customs Inspector from the federal government. The official stated that he required access to the 'airside' of the facility, to carry out checks in relation to a drug smuggling operation his department were currently investigating.

What the airport director could not have known was that Pierre Dubreton was in fact one of many carefully crafted aliases associated with this individual, the current one being supported by DRC customs documentation and a French passport. Dubreton was in fact in the employ of Bectel Inc. and was a clever, calculating and highly skilled assassin. Known simply as 'Gogol', he reported only to Stanley Harding, Bectel's Director of Intelligence and Security, his true identity a closely guarded secret known only to three men, the others being Max Simpson and Becker himself.

Born Uri Hazan in central Jerusalem in 1956, he grew up fighting for his survival in the ghettos of his beloved city.

At 18 years of age, he put his accumulated street knowledge and patriotic love of his country to good use and enlisted in the Israeli armed forces, where he quickly came to the attention of the Chief of MOSSAD, the Israeli counter terrorism and intelligence service, renowned throughout the world.

At just 20 years of age, Hazan played a pivotal role in the Israeli commando storming of the Air France, A300 Airbus at Entebbe Airport in Uganda in 1976. Escalating quickly through the ranks thereafter, he eventually attained the rank of Commander of the 7th Armoured Brigade, a military formation of the Israeli Defence Forces Northern Command, a position he relished until his retiral with full military honours in 2001. Throughout his entire time in the service, Hazan never married. A tall, handsome man with an athletic build, he had a string of relationships with women, however he viewed a wife and a family as a potential security risk and a means by which he could be coerced to give up his country's secrets, privileged information which he guarded jealously.

Having previously been nominated personally by Harrison Becker as a 'person of interest', Bectel's intelligence service had kept track of Hazan's career path in the latter part of his service, in the full knowledge that his loyalty and patriotism to his country could never dissuade him from the path he had chosen. But now that he had retired, that was a different matter.

Stanley Harding had been given a direct and unambiguous instruction from the head of Bectel, 'to secure this man's services, no matter what the cost.' Secret meetings were arranged, discussions entered into and generous inducements were offered.

In the Spring of 2003, the man formerly known as Uri Hazan entered into the employment of Bectel's Intelligence and Security Division. The cost of this endeavour was also a closely guarded secret second only to the man's true, and carefully guarded identity. Now known simply as Gogol, only the three individuals who knew his identity were aware of the secretive and important role he would fulfil.

The airport director, who was just heading home for the weekend, passed the task of fulfilling Monsieur Dubreton's request to his security chief who was more than happy to guide the customs officer around the airport, as there were no more scheduled flights due in or out until Monday. Dubreton, examining the sparse flight schedule given to him by the security chief, identified an arrival due in later that evening.

"What is this?" he enquired in English, but with an unmistakable French accent, shoving the schedule under the security chief's nose and tapping the page in disbelief.

"Ahh," the chief replied. "This is most unusual. This is a light aircraft charter from Kinshasa, despatched to return a government official to the capital after some business at the new hospital complex being constructed just a way up the road," nodding his head in the general direction of Kisangani.

"Seems they had to charter this flight because the official returns home this evening, and the next scheduled aircraft out of here isn't until Monday."

"This is exactly the sort of thing my department is interested in." Dubreton barked at the man, the anger in his voice apparent. "It was fortunate for you that I chose today to carry out my inspection."

"I want this plane secured as soon as it lands and I want an interview room to speak with this pilot, and the aircraft does not move until it has been personally inspected and cleared by me," Dubreton demanded, his tone indicating that he was not at all happy with the apparent care free attitude of the officials in charge of this airport.

"Yes sir," the chief replied, feeling somewhat intimidated and acquiescing to the man's demands, picking up the small black telephone on his desk.

It was now 7.00pm and whilst Benjamin Ngoy and his host were approaching the OSIPS structure where he was about to experience some difficulties, a Cessna 172S light aircraft, specially chartered for his return journey, was landing at Kisangani Airport. Immediately the plane arrived at the departure gate, and on the orders of Inspector Dubreton, the pilot was detained and the plane seized for examination.

During the thirty-minute interview Dubreton gave the pilot, a native of the suburbs of Kinshasa, a hard time wildly casting allegations of the trafficking of contraband, all of which were fervently denied. Paperwork was scrutinised and the pilot was held until the aircraft could be inspected.

By 7.45pm, with no evidence of any criminality, the pilot was released to fuel and prepare his aircraft for his return journey with his government passenger. What the pilot did not know was that during the inspection, there had been a small dark package, the size of a cigarette packet, inserted into the engine compartment of the aircraft.

The package, strategically placed by Pierre Dubreton, contained a small amount of C4 explosive which was timed to detonate at 10.05pm local time, just over one hour into the return flight.

The following day, the Kinshasa national news channel reported on the death of government official Benjamin Ngoy, and that of the pilot who was transporting him, when the light aircraft in which they were travelling crashed in the Salong National Park, in central DRC. The reports went on to confirm that aircraft in which they had been travelling had been completely destroyed and although all of the wreckage had not yet been located, initial indication of the cause was suspected to be pilot fatigue.

About two weeks later Dr Marcus Heyburn, an American medic who was part of the Medicines Sans Frontiers organisation (MSF) carrying out humanitarian aid in DRC and his colleague Nurse Claire Booth, were travelling on the dirt track that passed as the main thoroughfare between Koie and Yamboyo in the Salong National Park.

They were engaged in the task of delivering and administering vaccines to the residents of the remote villages in the area, when their four-wheel drive truck was forced off the road into a shallow ditch by an over enthusiastic lorry driver coming in the opposite direction.

Due to the unusually hot weather the ditch was completely dry and dusty and as Heyburn got out to check his vehicle for damage he noticed a brown cylindrical object, about a metre long, lying in the reeds just a few metres from his jeep. He picked up the object which had a crease in its centre section causing a slight bend, but found it otherwise undamaged.

Heyburn opened the cylinder and noted that there appeared to be several sheets of rolled paper within. Pulling the contents partway out, he was able to peek at the documents and could clearly see that they were some sort of blueprints for a building or structure. Aware of the plane crash in the area involving a government architect a few weeks earlier, he thought that this may be some debris from the plane. He placed the object in his truck with the intention of alerting the authorities when he got back to Kinshasa, and continued with his task.

Chapter 7

Kiritimati, is an atoll in the northern line islands, being a part of the *Republic of Kiribati*, which is an independent island nation comprising of a group of 33 atolls located in a remote area of the Pacific Ocean.

Kiritimati, nowadays also known as *Christmas Island*, can be found in the mid Pacific, straddling the 180th meridian and at a location just 232 km north of the equator, approximately 2,150 km south of Honolulu in Hawaii and approximately 8,600 km due west of the south American continent. Several of the *Republic of Kiribati's* atolls contain modest human settlements and Kiritimati itself, even though it had been previously abandoned, is one such atoll which has enjoyed a steady population increase since the mid 1960's.

The population today stands at just under 7,400 people around half of which reside in Tabwakea, its largest village located at the northernmost tip of the island. The remainder of the population resides mostly in the smaller villages of London, Banana, and Poland, also located in the north of the island. The southeastern peninsula of Kiritimati is largely uninhabited. To facilitate travel and commerce for its inhabitants, modern day Kiritimati relies heavily on Cassidy International Airport which is a small facility located just north of Banana and comprises of only one runway, measuring just over two kilometres in length.

Kiritimati was once claimed by the British Empire, who in 1882 initiated the beginnings of a permanent settlement comprising mainly of coconut plantation workers and fishermen. In 1902, in an attempt to consolidate a permanent colony on the island, the British government granted a 99 year lease to the '*Levers Pacific*

Plantations Company', who planted in excess of 72,000 coconut palms on the island and introduced silver lipped pearl oysters into the adjacent lagoon. This settlement did not endure due to the effects of extreme drought, which was ultimately responsible for the destruction of seventy five percent of the coconut palms, causing the island to be abandoned in 1905. Additional attempts were made to re inhabit the island and harvest coconut palms in the intervening decades, however nature again intervened and these further attempts at colonisation were eventually abandoned in 1939.

Following the end of World War Two, there was a brief period of world peace and respite for the region however the advent of the Cold War, and the ensuing tensions between the United States of America and the then Soviet Union, resulted in Kiritimati being used as a test and development facility for nuclear bombs.

In the late 1950's operation 'Grapple' saw the British carry out explosive testing of nuclear bombs in the area, with the USA carrying out similar practices, with their operation 'Dominic' in the early 1960's. These activities, the effects of which were really not fully understood at the time, resulted in the development of cracks and fissure that severely weakened the earth's crust in the area, rendering Kiritimati extremely vulnerable to seismic activity, a phenomenon common in this part of the Pacific.

In January 2018, the United States Geological Survey (USGS), assisted by 'state of the art' satellite imaging techniques, identified Kiritimati as a site of major volcanic eruption risk. This was mainly due to it being located within an area of dynamic volcanic activity, often referred to as the 'Pacific Ring of Fire', an apt description for a region where volcanic activity was commonplace due to the constant movements of the geological plates supporting the Pacific Ocean basin. The 'Ring of Fire', studied by geologists worldwide, itself runs in a gigantic horseshoe shape from the Korean Peninsula all the way up the east side of the Asian Continent and over to North America, where it extends downwards right through to the southernmost point of the Andes in South America.

The USGS had calculated that the scarred landscapes of the island, the unfortunate heritage of its use in nuclear bomb tests, had left a legacy of fundamental weakness in the earth's crust. These weaknesses, when coupled with episodes of recent unprecedented geological activity, posed a significant threat of a large scale volcanic eruption, on a par with that which devasted Mount St Helens in Washington state in the northwest United States in 1980.

At a meeting of the G7 group of countries in early 2018, it was concluded that although the risk of disaster could not be completely eliminated, consolidation of the island by 'infilling' would reduce the possibility of immanent eruption from 70% to 14% and although the projected costs would be astronomical, the task was deemed a global priority.

In mid May of 2018, the contract to design and deliver the project was awarded to Bectel Inc, being one of the few global construction enterprises with the expertise, resources and the financial backing to tackle such a momentous task.

Work began in early 2019 and by the late autumn of 2021 the project had been completed, with all the former fissures being repaired bringing, as the USGS monitoring devices would later confirm, 'geological stability' to the area.

As part of the stabilisation process, the cost of which was in excess of 180 billion US dollars, Bectel engineers had constructed a 200m high, three-sided pyramid in the remote south east of the island, the perceived epicentre of the weaknesses.

Constructed of 5m thick reinforced concrete, the pyramid

structure was deliberately built over a weak point in the crust, that was purposefully engineered into the repair programme. In simple terms the pyramid structure was meant to be akin to a gigantic pressure release valve, with the design implication being that any geological eruptions in the area would be channelled through cleverly designed 'arteries' in the infill process, up inside the pyramid where mechanisms inside would delay a full-scale volcanic eruption, providing precious time to affect an island wide evacuation.

Completed in Autumn 2021 and code-named *White Horse* by its owners, the Kiritimati pyramid was now under the control of Bectel's Intelligence and Security Division. In actuality, but known to very few people, the *White Horse* structure was identical in every detail to those that were under construction in other parts of the world.

As far as the USGS and the rest of the world were meantime concerned, the pyramid would now become a silent sentinel, quietly guarding against the incidence of a major catastrophic eruption, allowing island life to carry on as normal however to its creators, the structure would now lay dormant awaiting the time when its deadly purpose would be revealed.

Chapter 8

On the opposite side of the world to Kiritimati, concern was being expressed over the population of Indonesia which had been expanding exponentially over the last 60 years and as a consequence of such rapid growth, so did its desire for energy. In past years, government red tape and endemic corruption made it almost impossible to secure western investment, which was widely viewed by many in the region as the key to effective economic expansion.

After the fall of the 'New Order' in 1998 and the sweeping political reforms that followed, each of Indonesia's 34 provinces, collectively home to more than 270 million people, were given limited autonomy on how they governed their own part of the puzzle, with the proviso that any such leadership would conform to the federal governments broad encompassing guidelines. To say all corruption in public office had been eradicated would be grossly inaccurate however it certainly was now easier to get things done than it had been previously, especially if money and influence were present in the mix.

So it was with the city of Pontianak, the capital of the West Kalimantan province of the country, positioned directly on the Equator and located on the west coast of the island known to the world as Borneo, itself encompassing a population of over 23 million people.

In the summer of 2018, Bectel had tendered for the contract to build a power station to supply the energy needs of the rapidly expanding population of West Kalimantan. Following fierce local debate, and some early differences of opinion, the company were eventually awarded the contract and granted permission to construct their radically designed power generation facility which when completed was estimated to be capable of providing for the energy requirements of all of the Western Kalimantan region's five million inhabitants.

Located just 25km north of the capital Pontianak, the construction of the facility began in August 2019 and continued steadily without interruption until its completion in early November 2021.

Like similar structures recently constructed by Bectel, the power station was a gigantic three-sided pyramid, which rose 200m out of the equatorial jungle and like its identical sisters, one of the sides of the structure was aligned to face exactly due west. Within the Bectel organisation the Indonesian pyramid was codenamed *Pale Horse,* and when the news was confirmed that the structure was now complete, Harrison Becker permitted himself a wry smile of satisfaction.

The Indonesian governor of West Kalimantan, keen to capitalise on the political windfall the completed project represented, was eager to tap into the energy the Power Station would supply, and although disappointed that this energy was not immediately forthcoming, he was satisfied with the answer from Bectel that, stress testing, safety trials and commissioning having to be completed first, the energy generators would not go live until 5.37pm local time on 20th March 2022, just a few short months hence.

In the meantime, the pyramid was handed over to Bectel's Intelligence and Security Division, who until that date would maintain tight control of the structure, and more importantly the technology housed within.

Chapter 9

Harrison Becker was the CEO and genius entrepreneur behind the success of *Bectel Incorporated*, a global conglomerate he built up from the moderate beginnings of Becker Telecommunications, the first company he founded, drawing heavily on his lifetime of hard earned business acumen.

Bectel Incorporated was currently valued at 1.7 trillion US dollars, with Becker himself estimated to possess a personal fortune in excess of over 500 billion, a measure of success it would be difficult for anyone to deny.

Born in Austria in 1963, Harrison was the only child of Klaus Leon Becker, the billionaire shipping magnate and his young wife Marianne Mason, a mathematics professor and lecturer on the international circuit. They met at a conference in January of 1962 and, following a whirlwind romance, were married in the late spring of that year setting up home in Vienna. The following January their son and only child was born.

Moving to Texas when he was just ten months old, young Harrison became a naturalized American citizen and thereafter held dual nationalities.

Whilst living at the family ranch in Texas, Klaus Becker diversified into the oil business, which naturally led to the expansion of his tanker fleet, and by implication his fortune also. This rapid growth consumed almost all of his attention leaving little time for family life, a situation which ultimately came with a price tag.

In July of 1965, when Harrison was only two years old, his Mother Marianna took her own life, succumbing to a self-induced cocktail of drugs and alcohol in what was later diagnosed to be a form of delayed post-natal depression from which, despite the family's enormous wealth, she could not bring herself to rise above.

Klaus Becker did not attend his wife's funeral due to what he claimed were 'urgent business commitments', leaving his infant son to represent the family and for the child to look to his governess for emotional support. Several years later Klaus Becker would be heard to refer to the untimely death of his wife as a 'business inconvenience' as he carried on regardless with his expansion plans, arranging a succession of nanny's and tutors to support his son on the many occasions he was absent from the Texas Ranch on business. On the rare occasions when he was at home, Klaus tried to instil values *he* deemed important into young Harrison, values that would enable him to become a powerful and successful businessman, just like himself.

In the July of 1973, when Harrison was just ten years old and still living at the ranch in Texas, his father, in what was thought to be a rare display of thoughtfulness, bought him a golden Labrador puppy, which Harrison immediately fell in love with and named 'Jake'.

Over the following months the boy utterly adored his companion spending more and more time with the dog, exploring the enormity of the ranch in between school and private tutoring sessions at home.

In July 1974, on what was Jakes first birthday, Klaus Becker took his son to an outbuilding on the ranch where inside Jake was tied by his lead to a wooden support pillar.

Happy to see his young master, Jake began to wag his tail and strain at the lead. As Harrison went to move towards his pet to release him, his father put his hand across his son's chest preventing him from approaching the dog.

"Harrison," he said sternly. "You know you are leaving the ranch tomorrow to attend boarding school in the UK?" his mien suddenly adopting a stern and foreboding look. Klaus Becker was referring to Harrison's long planned attendance at Gordonstoun school in Scotland, where his preparations for greatness would begin in earnest.

Gordonstoun School was renowned for its standards, and for turning wealthy boys into wealthy men and those men into even wealthier 'Captains of Industry' and a few of those Captains into world leaders. Among the notable alumni of the school were both Prince Phillip Mountbatten, Royal consort and late Husband of Queen Elizabeth II, and his son, Charles III, the recently crowned King of the United Kingdom, following the death of his mother, Queen Elizabeth II.

Klaus Becker knew full well the value of networking and the advantages of a healthy address book, reasoning that contacts Harrison would establish at Gordonstoun would prove invaluable in later life, hence his choice of such an exclusive educational establishment for his young son.

In response to his father's reminder of his immanent departure from the ranch, young Harrison replied; "Yes sir, and I am so looking forward to it," he replied. Young Harrison, having spent most of his life in adult company, was anything but naive and wondered just where this conversation was heading.

"By the time you return from school, in eight years or so from now, Jake will be an old dog, and will probably have forgotten you," Klaus Becker said, in a tone that conveyed no comforting emotions for his son whatsoever.

"What I'm trying to say Harrison," he continued, "is that I am teaching you the first rule of business, and that is not to get emotionally attached to anybody or anything, as emotions are destructive entities which have the potential to impair your judgment."

"I think," his father went on, "it will be extremely detrimental to your education for you to be worrying about Jake whilst you are at Gordonstoun," his rhetoric building up to a horrifying climax.

"Harrison." he said. "Jake has served his purpose and has been your faithful companion for almost a year now, and it is time for you to say goodbye." As he spoke, Klaus Becker produced a 9mm automatic pistol from an inside pocket of his tweed jacket and offered it to the boy.

Leaping to a shocking conclusion Harrison cried out; "You are asking me to shoot Jake?" horrified at what his father was not only asking, but insisting that he do.

"I'm sorry Harrison but it is necessary," he said decisively.

"Because you have become so attached to each other, as soon as you leave Jake will pine and suffer, and I cannot have you worrying about that to the detriment of your education and your future destiny."

"This is the only way. Quick and clean, and it will be best for both of you."

Klaus Becker spoke with the same cold dispassionate resolve he demonstrated immediately following the death of Harrison's Mother and, although he was only two years old at the time, sinister echoes of his father's emotional detachment leapt to the forefront of the boy's conscious.

Tears welled up in young Harrison's eyes as he yelled at his father; "Why did you get me a dog in the first place?"

"I did it Harrison so that, when the time was right, I would be able to teach you a valuable lesson and that lesson is that 'emotion' is the adversary of the successful businessman. To succeed as a world leader, which one day you will be, you must be able to purge all emotion from your business decisions, ensuring that your judgement remains untainted."

Conflicting sentiments coursed through Harrison's young brain. Yes, he wanted to be a success in business and true, he was going away for some time and Jake would miss him as much as he would miss Jake. That part of his father's disconcerting advice was true. Awash with despair and confusion, and naively believing his father's counsel was in *his* best interests, he reluctantly took the weapon and approached Jake who greeted him enthusiastically.

Whilst he cuddled his canine friend for the last time, he placed the weapon against the skin of Jakes throat, and pointing the weapon upwards and away from himself, he pulled the trigger.

The animal died instantly and lay still in a small pool of blood, still attached by his lead to the wooden pillar. Harrison threw down the gun and ran from the outbuilding, tears blurring his vision, making for the sanctity of his bedroom in the main house where he locked the door on the world and his unimaginable grief.

Harrison Becker left for Gordonstoun the following day and spent the next eight years in Scotland, furthering his education and widening his cadre of influential acquaintances. In all the time he was at school in the UK his father never visited once, communicating with him infrequently by telephone. Following his graduation from school aged 19, he went on to attend Cambridge university, 1982 being his freshman year, where he studied Business Administration, Technology and Geology, graduating with Honours at aged 24, five short years later.

After his graduation, he returned to the family home in Texas where in 1987 he started a small telecommunications business, which he named 'Becker Telecommunications', and as it became successful, he later abbreviated to *Bectel* which as a business, with his insatiable ambition as the driving force, quicky expanded.

Harrison's company thereafter diversified into Civil Engineering and Construction, using his capital to take over existing companies, where he quickly mastered the intricacies of the various disciplines of each new business he subsumed. This led to interests in other fields, where to each he would inject his own style and flare recognising, utilising and rewarding the expertise of those he worked with, and in doing so expanded his business portfolio rapidly.

In 1997, just ten short years later, he consolidated all of his accumulated individual business interests into *Bectel Incorporated*, and in doing so became an icon of the *American Dream,* featuring on the cover of 'Time Magazine', whilst simultaneously expanding into the shipping business in direct competition with his father.

Two years later, in 1999 having outbid his father on all of his shipping contracts and driving his father's company stock prices into the ground, he led and was successful in a hostile takeover of Klaus Becker's shipping business, and in doing so made quiet reference to that lesson he was taught so long ago, by the man for whom now he felt nothing but contempt.

Following the takeover, Harrison Becker and his father ceased communications with each other completely, with the eventual outcome that Harrison Becker never saw his father again.

As Klaus Becker's stock prices continued to plummet, he tried unsuccessfully to prop up his company with his own personal fortune which was no match for the power and influence of

Bectel Incorporated's colossal financial assets, which his son Harrison now wielded with unrelenting destructive focus.

Soon afterwards, and finding himself financially destitute, Klaus Becker was shunned by those he once called friends and close business associates, and in a bitter twist of irony, on 17 March 2000, at his Texas ranch on an overcast Autumn morning, Klaus Becker put a pearl handled .38 antique revolver in his mouth, and pulled the trigger.

When he heard the news of his father's suicide, Harrison, Becker was dispassionately unmoved referring to the incident as a 'business inconvenience'. Taking little time to consider the situation he instructed a senior member of his legal team to make all the necessary funeral arrangements, a funeral, he instructed, "that he would not be attending."

Chapter 10

Some years later, around mid-September 2016, with Bectel Inc. at the pinnacle of its power and influence, Harrison Becker, a keen ecologist and long term 'friend of the earth', met with the Chinese Premier Hin Shi Wan. The meeting took place at the Presidential Palace of the PRC in Beijing, for talks on what was being presented outwardly to the world's media as a range of communal business interests.

Becker, being a person of interest to the CIA meant that Bectel was prominent on their 'radar' with Becker himself under constant surveillance, consequently the Americans were not convinced on the 'communal business interests' story, suspecting it to be a cover for some sort of nefarious activity. The CIA's primary concern at the time was that the meeting was a front for what they suspected to be some sort of communist collaboration, and they were open to the possibility that Bectel had been commissioned by the Chinese government, who it was known, were looking to acquire a new type of propulsion system for space travel. Previous intelligence had indicated that Bectel engineers had secretly been working on such a project.

What the CIA did not know however was that they themselves were being covertly monitored by Bectel's Intelligence and Security Division, who were leaving a set of subtle clues on that very topic, for CIA covert operatives to uncover and report back on. The laying of these clues was part of a carefully scripted counterintelligence plot that would give the Americans something tangible to follow, masking the true purpose of the meeting.

The lead up to the audience with the Chinese stemmed back

to when Becker, having nurtured a keen interest in worldwide ecology and conservation since his youth, was extremely concerned about the imminent threat of global warming and the effect it was having on the planet. Following extensive research from his intelligence division, Becker regarded the Chinese, with their rapid expansion and development plans, as the main contributors to this destructive phenomenon and the body least likely to compromise.

The talks did in fact primarily centre around several business proposals in various fields that were designed to induce the Chinese to cut their Carbon Dioxide emissions, with a view to combating global warming, in return for access to Bectel's innovative working practices. Included was indeed an inducement to share in the roll out of a new secret propulsion system for spacecraft, that Bectel was in the process of developing, which when completed would undoubtedly support the Chinese ambition of putting the first human on the surface of Mars.

Becker kept the information he was sharing to a minimum, but in essence what he was offering would reduce the current six-month journey time to Mars to a mere six weeks, and to the Moon in just hours. After three days the talks concluded with no concessions from the Chinese side and no agreement on a strategy to combat the global warming phenomenon, despite the offer of the chance to beat the USA to Mars.

On the 20th September 2016, Becker returned disenchanted to his private yacht, where he immediately convened a meeting with Maxwell Simpson, his steadfast deputy CEO.

"Well Max," he said to his second in command, in the boardroom of the yacht currently anchored in the Yellow Sea just off the west coast of the Korean Peninsula.

"Let history show that I tried."

"That you did sir," Simpson retorted sympathetically, in support of his bosses currently vexed state of mind.

"I think we have no option here Max!" "We need to teach these people a lesson in humility before it's too late therefore I want you to begin immediately on the contingency we had discussed for this eventuality, should the Chinese refuse to give way."

"Unfortunately, it will take some time to reach a state of immanent readiness for our new focus to be effective, so it is imperative that we begin immediately."

"Your instructions sir?" Simpson asked, poised and ready to carry out his bosses wishes to the letter, no matter what.

"First," Becker began. "Get onto Tim Allen at Aerospace Division. I want all work on the Trans Warp Propulsion System put on hold, and his entire division diverted to supporting our new goal."

"Next, get a hold of Stanley Harding at Intel and give him the heads up on what is coming. His department are going to be busy. Tell him I want an up-to-date security vetting check on all departmental directors immediately, and I want the results by breakfast time tomorrow." The tone that Harrison Becker adopted with his number two implied that there was no room for ambiguity in these instructions.

"Then Max, I want you to summon all the department directors to a meeting at our HQ in Mendi. They will be coming from around the world so give them time to get there and settle in. Set the date appropriately, but no more than five days from now."

"And finally, tell the Captain to get this boat moving. I want to get to HQ and have time to prepare. Make it happen Max!" he ordered.

"Yes sir, of course sir," Simpson replied, marching purposefully off towards his office in a different part of the vessel.

Simpson knew the scale of what Bectel was about to embark on, uppermost in his mind being the knowledge that the instructions he had just been given were unequivocal, and it was now his sole responsibility to ensure they were carried out to completion. Within an hour of being instructed to do so, Max Simpson had carried out his CEO's wishes and summoned the directors of each of Bectel's six divisions, to what was likely to be the most important meeting any of them had ever attended.

Commensurate with Becker's wishes, the meeting was scheduled to take place at 10.00am on 23 Sept 2016, just three days hence and at Bectel's HQ, a cathedral sized chamber carved out of solid rock in the mountains just east of Mendi, in Papua New Guinea.

Becker had commissioned the structure some five years previously and equipped it with every modern convenience available, including state of the art communications facilities, an aircraft landing strip and a helicopter pad. What was essentially a small town inside a mountain, this was the Headquarters of Bectel Incorporated, and the home of Bectel's Intelligence and Security Division. It was, for all intents and purposes a fortress, impregnable to any form of cyber, electronic or physical attack.

Three days later, his yacht moored in the aptly named 'Deception Bay', located to the south of Papua New Guinea, Harrison Becker stood at the head of the conference table in the boardroom of Bectel Inc. HQ, as he addressed his executives with the usual calm unflappable demeanour that was his hallmark.

"Ladies and gentlemen. Welcome to *The Citadel*, our corporate headquarters, and epicentre of Bectel's International operations. For most of you it will be your first time here. I trust your quarters are comfortable and that your individual needs have been catered for?"

Affectionately nicknamed 'the pencil' among his divisional directors, as his initials resembled that of the universally popular graphite writing implement, Harrison Becker's remarkable success was in part due to the fact that ever since his first foray into the world of business, he always knew how to look after his people. What he had just referred to as comfortable quarters for his employees would easily pass for five-star accommodation in any of the world's top city hotels.

Becker, continuing with his introduction, went on;

"As you are all aware, we have been engaged in the secret development of a Trans Warp Propulsion System for some time now, in an effort to assist humankind in their quest to populate other worlds, and therefore ensure the survival of the human race."

"Likewise, you will all be aware of my ongoing and extensive efforts to preserve the resources that we already have here on Earth." Becker's elite audience generated some positive mumblings and spontaneous head nodding at these comments. "In furtherance of our organisation's global aspirations, I have recently approached the Chinese government, who are by far the largest contributors to the phenomenon known as global warming and despite my best diplomatic efforts to induce them to reduce their carbon emissions by sharing our practices and our innovative technology, they have refused me."

"In summary, and after much deliberation on how best to pursue this situation, we as a company have no option but to take matters into our own hands. So, for the foreseeable future Bectel, through your respective divisions, will focus wholly and exclusively on the top-secret project, I am now about to share with you."

The meeting sat in silence, transfixed on their CEO's every word with awe and trepidation. Rumour had spread amongst the executive team that Bectel was about to embark on a 'something big', and each one of the handpicked divisional directors were about to be entrusted with the enormity of just what that project would entail.

Harrison Becker took to the floor and for the next two hours, with the aid of various state of the art presentational tools, captivated his staff with his vision of what was now Bectel's top priority project, to which he assigned the codename;

project *Chrysalis*

Although there was a wealth of academic, technical and engineering expertise gathered around the table, not one of them had imagined what was being proposed was even possible, let alone what they were now being tasked to support. The assembled executive knew however that Harrison Becker would not make such a bold proposal lightly, and each and every one of them knew that the fact that 'the Pencil' was now discussing the subject in this exclusive forum, signified that it was about to happen.

Chapter 11

Construction of the new entertainment venue in Ecuador was falling behind schedule.

It was now June 2021 and although the re-elected Varas government was keeping up their end of the Bectel investment arrangement as best as they could, the powerful drug cartels were seriously interfering with the progress of the structure, located due west of the country's capital.

The *Inca Cartel,* by far the most powerful and feared of the Ecuadorian drug gangs, was the dominant player on the drug scene. They were responsible for producing most of the country's Heroin and Cocaine, distributing it not only locally but also throughout neighbouring Columbia and on into the United States, where their product was aggressively marketed.

The *Inca* leader was an uncompromising individual who's birthname was Santiago Torres however he was known exclusively by everyone in Ecuador as *'La Serpiente'*, the Serpent. At 34 years of age, Torres had risen quickly through the ranks of drug traffickers and enforcers to make his way to the *Inca* throne, and now enjoyed the reputation as the most merciless and feared drug lord in Ecuador.

The Serpent's reputation for ruthlessness was justly deserved. It was at his behest that the execution of an entire village of men, women and children was brought about, merely because someone in the village was suspected of tipping off the authorities as to the location of a drug production lab in the north west of the country, which was subsequently located and destroyed by the authorities. It was widely understood by all in Ecuador that anyone who crossed or displeased *La Serpiente,* usually ended up with a bullet in their head.

More recently, and on the direct instructions of the Serpent, the *Inca* drug cartel were intimidating workers and disrupting the flow of raw materials, necessary for the completion of the new auditorium being built just outside Quito. This was a brazen attempt to extort large sums of money from the development company, the name of whom the Serpent could not even be bothered to recall.

Having presided over his turf for over four years, The Serpent had no real idea of who or what Bectel was, nor did he care. His word in this territory was absolute, and no one would dare to challenge him. If any threat to his supremacy existed at all, he often pondered to himself, it was most likely to come from inside his own organisation.

It was this belief in his own invincibility that fuelled the arrogance of the Serpent, who had expressed little concern over the request to convene a private meeting with a Bectel representative, who had boldly made the request in an attempt to further both organisations 'mutual interests'.

Word on the street was that the construction company were prepared to capitulate and make a financial tribute to the *Inca's,* in exchange for the unhindered completion of their project, and speculation hinted that a price tag of one million US Dollars was being considered. The Serpent was, in principle, prepared to accept such a payment and step back, as the completion of the new entertainment venue would serve to provide an influx of people from all over the world, essentially consolidating the *Inca's* ambitious business expansion plans.

The meeting was secretly arranged and took place at a private villa in the mountains southwest of Quito, a place where the Serpent felt secure. In the bright morning sunshine of 29th June 2021, a black S class Mercedes saloon with one occupant, approached the secret villa nominated for the rendezvous. The vehicle was stopped at the gatehouse to the property and thoroughly searched before being waved through the security gate and directed up the lightly inclined driveway towards the main residence.

At the top of the driveway the vehicle was met by *los dientes de la Serpiente,* 'the teeth of the Serpent', the *Inca* leader's most trusted bodyguards, every one of whom was a blood relative.

The occupant of the Mercedes, who was smartly but casually dressed in a white linen suit, muslin shirt and casual loafers, stepped out into the sunshine and was immediately searched for weapons and electronic surveillance devices. The aluminium briefcase he was carrying when opened revealed a large amount of American dollars, packed in neat bundles. Having carried out a cursory search of the item, both the man and his luggage were escorted inside the building where he was introduced to the Serpent as Rodriguez Moralez, Bectel's Ecuadorian project liaison officer.

The Serpent grunted his disdain for the man, at the same time indicating a degree of tolerance of his presence, at least for the moment. Motioning him to follow, the Serpent headed into the main residence.

What the Serpent could not possibly have known was that the man was no other than Gogol, an assassin from Bectel's Intelligence and Security Division, and he had only one purpose in attending this meeting, and that was the advancement of Bectel's interests by the elimination of Santiago Torres, and anyone with any close associations to him.

Senior Moralez gratefully accepted the offer of a cup of coffee made by his host and in very broken English, grunted rather than spoken, the Serpent made a pitiful attempt at conversation. The men then moved through to the main lounge of the residence where the cool sanctity of the large room and comfortable surroundings were a welcome relief from the scorching temperatures outside. Much to Moralez's satisfaction, several ceiling fans were in operation in the room helping circulate the humid air. "Excellent," he thought quietly to himself. "This will suit my purpose very well."

As his four bodyguards, positioned themselves around the room, weapons relaxed but still held in readiness, the Serpent motioned for Moralez to sit, and so commenced the main business of the meeting.

Draining his coffee cup and placing it on a nearby table, Moralez began. Although fluent in Spanish, Gogol withheld this skill from the persona of Rodriguez Moralez, hoping the Serpents complacency would lead him to relax and perhaps let slip his true intentions to his guards in their own language, giving Gogol the advantage of the element of surprise. As Moralez started speaking, slowly and in English, one of the guards translated his words into Spanish for the Serpent.

"I have here, a token of good will from my company." Moralez began, opening the case and turning it towards the Serpent, revealing the contents to be a large quantity of American Dollars, neatly sectioned off in $10,000 bundles.

"This is an unconditional personal gift to you and your organisation," he continued, stalling each sentence until the translation was delivered.

"There is one million US dollars in this suitcase as an incentive for you to consider a cessation of your activities, disruptive actions that are detrimental to my company's progress in the construction of the entertainment auditorium, just west of Quito," adding "Which I believe lies within your territory, and that you may be familiar with."

Performing the role of Rodriguez Moralez perfectly, Gogol had introduced an element of nervousness into his voice to suit the character, but at the same time he tried to convey that this amount of money was but a mere trifle to him, which in actuality was not far from the truth, as Gogol himself possessed a personal fortune of over two hundred million dollars.

The Serpent sat silent and unmoved, sipping delicately at his coffee cup, his dark, dangerous eyes giving no indication as to what treacherous thoughts were flashing through his mind.

Moralez continued. "With your agreement," he said, "Bectel will deliver the same amount of cash to you, at a location of your choice every month until the pyramid structure west of Quito is fully completed." Pausing until the translation was delivered, Moralez expected some form of acknowledgment of the enormity of the financial sums that were on offer. A smile perhaps, a grin even. He was however disappointed as the Serpent sat still and unmoved.

Forcing himself to go on Moralez said, "All we ask in return is that the local labour force be permitted to continue attending the site without fear of retribution and that we are permitted to continue unmolested with our deliveries of construction materials necessary to complete our project," adding, "And that you extend your influence to prevent others from doing likewise," referring to the other rival criminal gangs.

The Serpent, aptly named for his reputation as a ruthless, double dealing untrustworthy individual, considered what was being offered for a moment and as the translation caught up, now grinning menacingly, he nodded to the bodyguard who had been translating.

Replying in his local dialect, speaking rapidly in order that the stranger would not be alerted to his intentions, he delivered his determination.

Moralez of course had picked up the Serpents deceitful comments, but perpetuating the illusion that he did not understand the language, he looked towards the guard expectantly awaiting the translation.

"*La Serpiente* accepts your tribute Senior Moralez, and will agree to the terms of your proposal," said the bodyguard.

What the bodyguard did not say however is that the Serpent had decreed that once the venue was complete, his boss intended to control the flow of patrons to the structure at which point the tribute would increase significantly or this 'pyramid' would become nothing more than an expensive oversized landmark.

In keeping with his character, Moralez let out a huge sigh of relief and as the Serpent nodded his approval, confirming the terms of the deal, his men in the background, who had been poised and ready to eliminate the visitor at the merest blink of an eye from their boss, relaxed from a state of readiness and fully lowered their weapons. These four men, plus two others at the gate were the Serpents most trusted and loyal employees, and as well as each one being related by blood to their boss in some way, each was also a ruthless killer who would obey their kinsman without question. The Serpent kept his close bodyguard small in number as it was the only way he could ensure absolute fealty.

The business seemingly concluded the Serpent and Moralez shook hands sealing the deal, at which point the casually dressed Bectel representative requested the use of the washroom prior to his departure. As Moralez left the room, the Serpent and his entourage gathered around the briefcase where the Serpent, grinning ominously, started handing out bundles of cash to his kinsmen.

Meanwhile in the washroom and with no time to lose, Moralez, who had now reverted to the persona of Gogol, rolled up a linen towel and soaking it in the wash basin, placed it along the bottom of the washroom door. He then unwound the crown of his Breitling Superchronomat watch, and pulled it out one stop. With the crown still in this position, he pressed both additional function buttons on the timepiece simultaneously.

In the lounge of the villa, just a few metres away, a colourless odourless nerve agent known as VX, was injected into the atmosphere from hidden panels within the opened attaché case and within seconds, assisted by the ventilation fans, the Serpent and his four Kinsmen all of whom had been gathered greedily around the case, lay unconscious on the villa floor, gasping their final breaths.

Taking two specially adapted cigarettes from a case in his breast pocket, Gogol snapped off the filter tips from the ends and pushed one filter tip up into each of his nostrils. Gogol knew that, providing he kept his mouth closed, these carefully designed and specially treated filters would allow him to breath until the deadly nerve gas, which he had just unleashed on his host, had dispersed.

Re-entering the lounge and taking a large hunting knife from one of the Serpent's guards, Gogol slit the throats of each of the four, armed men whose lives rapidly bled out onto the marble floor. Using the same knife Gogol turned to the Serpent and fully decapitated him, placing his severed head in a plastic bin liner and, having retrieved the money and the attaché case, made his way out to his Mercedes, its black paintwork gleaming in the south American sunshine.

Placing the decapitated head in the front passenger footwell of the vehicle, Gogol sat behind the wheel in a casual manner, trying not indicate to the men at the gate, who were now in the final seconds of their life, what had just taken place a few moments before.

The Mercedes negotiated the central courtyard and headed tentatively down the driveway towards the front gate and as it did so, Gogol operated a switch causing both headlamps to flip downwards to reveal a rocket propelled grenade and launcher behind each unit. At the press of a button on the dashboard, both RPG's shot towards the gatehouse 50 metres away, instantly destroying it and the two *Inca* guards that were standing beside it.

As the black Mercedes sped away through the smoke and the debris, Gogol dialled a number on the satellite car phone and spoke with his immediate superior and head of Bectel security, Stanley Harding.

"Sir," he said with no hint whatsoever of any stress or anxiety in his voice. "It is Gogol reporting that your problem in Ecuador has been eliminated."

"Thank you, my friend," replied Harding. "Never doubted it for a moment."

Although he was Gogol's superior, he had never actually met the man and decided then that he would never want to. Harding concluded the conversation. "Please ensure the package gets delivered as discussed, and make your way to your extraction location where a plane will be waiting."

"Yes sir," Gogol replied, ending the call.

The following morning, the chief editor of the local national newspaper 'El Mundo' received a hat box sized package at his office. He opened the box and was both surprised and appalled at what the box contained.

The main story that evening was the death and brutal decapitation of the feared drug lord *La Serpiente* and his entire personal bodyguard, in a villa up in the mountains. The article spoke of the power vacuum this killing would create, anticipating a turf war that would have the rival gangs in Ecuador fighting each other for years to come.

Chapter 12

Grant Steven Wilson was born in Scotland UK, in July 1988 into an unremarkable but otherwise, ethical and hard-working family. His sister Jasmine was just three years older, and took it upon herself to act as guardian and protector of her younger sibling. This would be the case right up until Jasmine's teenage years, when the onset of puberty took all of her emotions and mixing them up, removed all reason and logic from her 'complicated' life, leaving her to suffer the fate of almost every teenage girl in western society until around age twenty-one, when magically and mysteriously, sanity and calm would return to her world.

Living just outside of Glasgow, Scotland's largest city, young Grant had an ordinary upbringing in a small village just to the north of the ever-expanding city boundary. He underwent an education that was typical for a boy from a working-class background and did all the usual things that boys of his age would normally do, in particular the playing of computer games, a pastime at which he excelled. Possessing the unusual ability to 'second guess' the gaming parameters of the virtual worlds he would enter, Grant was adept at achieving top level scores in any game he turned his attention to.

It wasn't until the first year of Grant's high school education, when he was aged just twelve, that his parents were summoned to a meeting by Grant's guidance teacher, Mr McKinney, who had noticed the child's unusual academic abilities. Grant, although very competent in mathematics, physics and the sciences displayed an unusual aptitude for lateral thinking.

Following some candid experimentation with advanced

level, abstract thinking questions, Mr McKinney confirmed his suspicions of his pupil's extraordinary abilities and wrote to the boy's parents inviting them to a meeting. In his office on an overcast Thursday afternoon in early summer of 2000, Mr McKinney greeted Grants parents, Steven and Madelaine, with candid exuberance and explained that the reason for the summons was to discuss an alternative education path for their son.

Grant at this point remained outside the office, sitting in an armchair and staring out of the window studying the behaviour of the different species of birds, the names of which he could easily recall from memory, and suffering from a mild case of boredom.

Mr McKinney went on to produce copies of Grants work in all of his subjects to his parents, but highlighted mathematics and the sciences as particularly good examples of how far ahead of his class he was. He then went on to discuss the post graduate university level problems he had candidly offered Grant to look at, and of how each and every one had been returned with textbook solutions.

"In fact," Mr McKinney added gleefully, "several of the scenarios returned by Grant had solutions that even the professors at the examination board, who had initially devised the questions, had not considered."

"In short," he said "Mr and Mrs Wilson, you have raised one supersmart individual who has a unique gift for lateral thinking, and with your permission I would like to subject Grant to a good old fashioned IQ test and then take it from there."

"I have absolutely no doubt," he went on, "that he will score highly but, even in his first year of high school, Grant has already shown that he possesses a highly intellectual thinking brain and I believe that it is our duty to nurture this gift and steer him towards the most appropriate pathway that will enable development of this unique ability." Delighted to hear such a glowing report of their son, Grant's parents agreed to further testing at which point Grant was summoned into his teacher's office.

"Grant," began Mr McKinney with a smile. "I have just been going over your work with your parents and telling them how pleased we are here at the school with the remarkable progress you are making."

Grant sat on a wooden chair beside his parents with his hands under his thighs, palms down on the seat and swinging his legs to and fro under the chair. He cracked a broad grin at the compliment.

"I would like, Grant," Mr McKinney continued, "with your permission of course, to have you complete an IQ test, which should give us a good idea about where to accurately pitch the level of education we have to offer you. Would you be willing to do this?"

Grant looked at his parents who nodded their approval.

"Dunno," he said. "I suppose so."

"Splendid," said Mr McKinney. "Leave it with me and I will make all the necessary arrangements."

Three weeks later Grant underwent independent IQ testing at his school, while the rest of his class were undergoing an afternoon of 'Speech and Drama'.

When the results of the testing came back, they exceeded even Mr McKinney's expectations indicating that Grant had an outstanding IQ of 159, which is well above the 99.9 percentile of the human population, putting Grants IQ at genius level and only one point below that of Albert Einstein, the renowned physicist and author of the 'theory of relativity'.

Young Grant however had his own ideas, and when he realised the implications of developing his superior intelligence, he flatly refused to pursue the lateral educational path that was being laid out before him, on the grounds that it would mean changing schools and leaving all of his friends and family behind. Despite the pleas from his guidance teacher and encouragement from the wider educational establishment, he dug his heels in and refused to move schools. In this respect, although bitterly disappointed at Grant's decision, his parents were very supportive and acquiesced to their sons wishes.

Grant therefore went on to complete his high school education easily and with distinction, graduating as his school's DUX student and highest achieving pupil ever. The inevitable next stage in his education saw him study Mathematics, Engineering, Physics and Chemistry at Glasgow university, where he excelled, before going on to pursue a longstanding career aspiration to become an officer in the British Royal Navy.

Grant Joined the Royal Navy in 2010 as an officer candidate, and during his multiple deployments on UK warships and submarines, his analytical skills were quickly acknowledged by his superiors, following which he quickly rose up through the ranks reaching the position of Commodore, just seven years later at age twenty nine.

This was one of Grants many accolades and was a task never before accomplished in the modern British Royal Navy's, three hundred year history.

The practical outcome of this outstanding performance was

his nomination, by none other than the UK Prime Minister, to fulfil the role of 'Head of Tactical and Strategic Analysis', based at Her Majesty's Naval Base, Clyde, on the Clyde estuary in Scotland, approximately 40 miles west of Glasgow.

It was whilst embedded in this role that Grant authored the Navy's *'Tactical and Cyber Warfare Response'* for the entire UK Fleet's 21st century warships and submarines, a work of distinction that would follow him throughout the rest of his Naval career.

Chapter 13

1 February 2022

Stanley Harding had been apprehensive about making this call but to delay any longer would only cause him more anguish than what he was currently experiencing.

Max Simpson was seated at his opulent desk in Bectel's Swiss office when the video call from the Director of Intelligence and Security was patched through.

"Yes Stanley, what can I do for you?" Simpson offered.

"Are you alone sir?" Harding enquired.

"Yes. You may speak freely," Simpson replied, sitting upright, his well-tuned senses instantly jumping to the alert.

"Sir, we have intercepted some 'chatter' that British Intelligence are showing interest in a house fire that occurred in the western DRC, back on 1st October 2021."

"Historical house fires are a little bit below their pay grade, aren't they?" Simpson remarked, adding sarcastically, "Have MI6 run out of government officials to spy on?"

"No sir," Harding replied, his demeanour stern. "The fire was in the newly built home of Nava Tumeli, the leader of the terrorist organisation, the CFF who control territory and operate in the west of the DRC."

"You will be aware we have had some trouble with Tumeli in the recent past, when he tried to intercept the flow of materials from the Port at Matadi, destined for the *Red Horse* site at

Kisangani.   It was our operatives that attacked him, killed his second in command along with his entire bodyguard, and burned his previous residence to the ground to convey the message that he and his organisation should back off."

"Also, as you know, Tumeli was only left alive in order that the message would propagate through his organisation and be a warning to others."

"Well sir, it would appear," Harding continued with his report, "that Tumeli and his entire family, including his 13 children, were completely incinerated in this blaze as there was not a trace of human flesh, or much else for that matter, left at the house."

"The only remaining body was one of his guards who, it would appear, tried to shelter from the inferno by jumping down a water well, and there is not much left of him either."

"Perhaps it was the work of one of Tumeli's rivals. I'm sure there would be a queue of people a mile long glad to see him dead?" Simpson offered up as a plausible explanation.

"Unlikely sir," Harding continued.   "Apparently military satellites, passing overhead at the time, detected a very bright flare in the area which they interpreted as a ballistic missile launch, following which a host of UK defence protocols were initiated involving three UK typhoon fighters being scrambled out of Nigeria and a UK nuclear submarine off the coast of Africa being put on high alert."

"It was only when the flare continued to burn that the defence status was reduced and latterly, after analysis, declared a false alarm, resulting in the fighters being recalled and the submarine stood down."

"And do we know the cause?" Simpson enquired, expecting a definitive answer.

"No sir, not at the moment, but we do know that the flare burned brightly for over twenty minutes and consumed everything within a two hundred metre radius of the property, turning it to ash. There is absolutely nothing left."

"Could it be an arms store that caused this?" Simpson again proffered as a logical explanation.

"Again, unlikely sir, as there were no reports of additional fires or explosions, a common characteristic of small ordinance detonations."

"The only definitive information we have was that the flare was very intense and uniform throughout the entire time of the incident, defying all attempts to extinguish it. Then it simply faded to the magnitude of a normal blaze before extinguishing itself, as if whatever was fuelling it, was suddenly spent."

"This is too close to *Red Horse* to be a coincidence," Max Simpson concluded with an uncharacteristic edge to his voice, "and although the structure is complete and secure, this incident is likely to attract unwanted government attention."

"Get a team over there immediately and get me a full report," Simpson instructed. "Mr Becker will want to know everything. I will expect your personal report to me in 24 hours."

"Yes sir," Harding replied nervously, visibly relieved as the call was terminated and the screen went blank.

At the other end of the call, Max Simpson stared at his own reflection in the blank screen in front of him for a moment, unable to distinguish his own features in the reflection. If that had been possible, he would have been able to discern the uncharacteristic signs of apprehension in his mien, as he composed himself to deliver the potentially worrying news to his superior.

A short time later Harrison Becker received the unwelcome

news aboard his luxury yacht via a video news brief from Max Simpson. Exhibiting the calm demeanour of a chess master who has anticipated his opponents every move, Becker sat within his office in the vessel in quiet deliberation, his hands clasped together in silent contemplation of his next move.

Max sat patiently, awaiting his superior's response. Finally, Harrison Becker spoke.

"What is the status of *Red Horse*?" he enquired, already knowing the answer and fully expecting Max to confirm it.

"The *Red Horse* facility is fully complete, secure and primed sir, and in the hands of our Security Division until the appointed time."

"Thank you, Max." Becker replied.

"Notwithstanding whatever your team uncovers in their pending report I deem *Red Horse* secure, prepared and impregnable."

"The time till ignition is drawing near and even a full government intervention now, unlikely as it is, would be fruitless."

Prior to terminating the call Harrison Becker issued instructions to his number two.

"Increase security at all sites just in case, and bring me your report from Africa as soon as you have it."

"Yes sir," Simpson replied, terminating the call, somewhat relieved at his boss's confidence.

Six hours later Stanley Harding's Intelligence team arrived at the Tumeli residence in Western DRC where the 'blaze' had occurred and, under the guise of government health and safety officials, carried out an inspection of the site. Their inspection lasted just under one hour, where they took photographs and some soil and rock samples. Four hours later they were at a safe house in the town of Caxito, just east of Luanda in neighbouring Angola, transmitting their report to Stanley Harding for onward transmission to Max Simpson, who just fifteen hours after being made aware of the incident was again briefing the head of Bectel.

"Sir, I have our Intel Divisions full report on the Tumeli incident and I am ready to update you at your convenience." Max Simpson relayed to his boss, via the usual secure video link.

"That would be now Max, thank you," Replied Becker. "Please proceed and omit nothing."

Max updated Harrison Becker with every shred of information he had acquired on the incident, including photographs and video footage, both at ground level and from an ariel perspective, courtesy of a drone. Both Harding and Simpson were particularly interested in the drone footage which showed the site from the air, where the images clearly showed an outline of the main parts of the newly built residence, which was until recently, a two-story mansion house.

"If I may sir?" Simson continued in his brief. "If you compare what you are looking at with the blueprint plans of the foundations of the Tumeli residence, which we were able to obtain from the local planning authority," which Simpson now superimposed on the screen, "you will see an exact match to the outline of the house."

"Analysis of this pattern has also revealed that the surrounding earth, adjacent to the structure's foundations has actually melted, due to the intensity of the blaze, changing the nature of the rock to something resembling cooled magma, similar to what one would expect to find at the site of a volcanic eruption."

"This we find to be somewhat unusual, as most of the fuel for the blaze would be the building materials used to construct the dwelling, and be above ground level."

"And your interpretation of this Max?" Becker enquired, attempting to assimilate what he was being told.

"From what I was able to ascertain in the time available sir," Simpson continued, laying the way for an excuse in case what he was about to say was insufficient to satisfy his boss, "is that we believe the foundations for Tumeli's new house may have been taken from a hi-jacked rail freight tanker, containing the propellant mixture for *Red Horse*, stolen somewhere between Matadi and Kisangani."

"Sources on the ground, who have subsequently been eliminated, have stated that Tumeli seems to have mistaken the propellant for liquid concrete and ordered his men to hijack one tanker load of the mixture, which he subsequently used as the foundations on which he built his property. The mixture set, as it would in a manner similar to concrete, and the build commenced as normal, with no issues until after completion."

"It was only when one of Tumeli's wives started a fire in a ground floor fireplace that the mixture reached flashpoint and caught light, igniting all of the subterranean foundations simultaneously, resulting in the flare that the American satellite observed. That fire instantly consumed the property and everything and *everyone* in it."

"The fire could not be extinguished by conventional means and only began to subside of its own accord when all of the propulsion fuel was spent. When the fire had gone out all that was left was ash, and the badly burned corpse of one of Tumeli's men, who apparently tried to seek shelter down a water well."

Continuing Simpson went on, "Local government officials

have been all over the site and have the remains of the body at a mortuary in Kinshasa. Unfortunately sir, British intelligence have also been at the site and taken soil and rock samples, as well as tissue samples from what was left of the body."

Again, Harrison Becker sat silently musing what he had just been told.

Max Simpson, on the opposite end of the screen, over seven thousand kilometres and four times zones away, sat poised and in readiness. After what seemed an eternity Becker rendered his determination.

"I am certain that in a short time, analysis of the corpse and artifacts from the site will indicate the cause, nature and intensity of the fire, and identify the compound responsible."

He continued; "Investigation will no doubt reveal where Tumeli acquired the compound and in the absence of an alternative logical explanation, the trail will lead directly to the *Red Horse* structure, therefore in order to keep the focus away from our project for as long as possible we must give the NATO alliance an alternative logical explanation for the fatalities."

"I want you to identify a similar terrorist organisation in the region, any one of Tumeli's rivals ought to do, and have Harding initiate an immediate terror campaign in their name. Destroy a few important buildings and a couple of villages and attribute the destruction to them. That ought to keep NATO busy and buy us the time we need until the Vernal Equinox, and the conclusion of our plans."

"Yes sir," said Simpson, snapping back into focus.

"And Max."

"Yes sir?" Simpson paused.

"I want you to instruct Harding to send Gogol over there to work on an adjacent mission."

"I think the elimination of a high profile, government official will also help shift the focus away from our plans."

"Have Gogol leave a subtle evidence trail that attributes the assassination to the Chinese. The Chinese will deny it of course, and the British will be tripping over themselves trying to be diplomatic about what they have discovered, and the subsequent 'tit for tat' round of diplomatic expulsions will keep them busy until it's too late."

"All noted sir," Simpson acknowledged.

"And Max," Harrison Becker added finally.

"Yes sir?" said Max attentively, waiting for the inevitable sting in the tail.

"I want you to remain distant from this. Gogol is to report directly, and only, to Harding."

"Yes sir," Max Simpson acknowledged as the call was terminated. It was only when the screen went blank that Max realised, he was perspiring.

Chapter 14

It was on an otherwise normal Friday morning on the 4th February 2022 and Commodore Grant Wilson was sitting at his desk, with a large cappuccino and a pile of reports to scrutinise, when his adjutant knocked on the door of his glass walled office.

"Sir," she began with usual naval brevity. "Top secret communication from *head office*," She said, using the accepted local slang term for the Admiralty at Naval Command HQ in Portsmouth England, some five hundred or so miles away. "You are required on the secure video link in the situation room straight away."

"Thank you, Lieutenant," he replied. "Find Commander Duffy and instruct her to attend there immediately, then grab a notepad and meet me there please," he said, gulping at his cappuccino.

"Yes sir," the Lieutenant replied, and went off to locate the base's second in command.

Ten minutes later Commander Karen Duffy, the bases OIC operations, entered the situation room where Wilson and his adjutant were waiting. There were several other Naval personnel of various subordinate ranks also in the room, working on routine intelligence tasks.

"May I have the room please?" Wilson said softly, but with sufficient intensity so that all other attendant personnel could hear his order, which was subtly disguised as a request.

The room was cleared and all three sat at a table facing a wall of video screens, the largest of which, with a screen size of 100 inches, was located in the centre of the array. The large screen displayed the Royal Navy logo which, at the press of a button on the table, faded out to reveal Admiral of the Fleet, Sir Durnian Cruickshanks, sitting at his desk in Portsmouth, his lavish office packed with many historical naval artefacts visible in the background.

"Good morning, Grant," said the Admiral, putting his pen back into its desk holder and sitting upright looking straight into the camera.

"Good morning, sir," Wilson replied on behalf of his team.

"Is the room secure?"

"Yes sir. The room is cleared and sealed, with only myself, Commander Duffy and Lieutenant Campbell present," adding, "the codec scrambler indicator is present on the screen, and your communication is confirmed as securely encrypted." Wilson was making reference to a small diamond shaped icon in the top, right hand corner of the screen which, when present, confirmed that the communication was being patched through Royal Navy encryption channels and was confirmed as being 'ultra-secure'.

"Bit of a flap going on down here," the Admiral began, in typical British Forces hierarchy fashion, grossly understating the situation.

"The defence minister has been on looking for our assistance. Seems that MI6 are getting all steamed up about some intel that our American cousins at the CIA have been pondering, which would appear to indicate something in the way of a global threat."

The Admiral was not one to engage in small talk and, as was his style, got right to the point.

"The PM," he said, using the accepted universal abbreviation which referred to the UK Prime Minister, "is convening an emergency meeting this evening to quantify this threat and wants an 'all hands on deck' approach," he added, using the age old navy analogy to convey the need for a large cadre of suitably qualified personnel to assist.

"What I am about to tell you and your team is top secret of course, and should not leave the room."

"It appears," the Admiral went on, "from what they can gather, there is concern about some sort of pyramid structures that have been 'popping up' around the globe."

"They are suggesting that these structures may be housing test facilities for some kind of advanced space propulsion system, that is being pursued on behalf of the Chinese or the Russians, and which could potentially give them the edge in space exploration, cutting spacecraft journey times to a fraction of what they are now."

"I don't have to tell you what that means if either of these two superpowers get a man on Mars first!" he said gruffly, coughing to clear catarrh from his throat, an unwelcome legacy of his cigar smoking days.

"The PM has asked for you in person," Cruickshank's announced. "Seems to think your particular skillset might lend a helpful perspective on how bad this could get, if what they have is correct."

"You are to report directly to the Minister for Defence at Whitehall, London, at 7.00pm this evening therefore I want you on a helicopter within the hour. Any issues?"

"No sir." Grant replied without hesitation. "Commander Duffy will take over here and I will get right on it."

"Good man," said the Admiral. "Thought you would."

"Now, as you know I am in my final year in the job and I don't want the RAF, Army intelligence or, God forbid, the CIA coming up with the answers on my watch, so get down there and do what you do best, in support of MI6. And don't forget to ensure that I am kept updated on your findings. You have my personal number," he reminded the Commodore.

"Yes sir," Wilson replied. "I won't forget." Grant immediately turned his thoughts to the overnight bag with some personal essentials, that he always kept packed and at the office, as these summons to detached duty were not an uncommon event. Otherwise, all that the current situation would require was a phone call home to his wife Julia, who would understand and who knew not to ask any questions.

Julia Wilson knew wholeheartedly that anything that prevented her husband's return to her at the end of the working day must be important, and was the small price she was willing to pay to be married to a decorated Naval Officer.

"Good luck Grant," the Admiral ended, softening his tone as a candid indication of the affection which he felt for the young officer. "Feel free to drop by if you can find the time. Cruickshanks out."

The Admiral ended with a press of a button, terminating the call and returning the screen to the Royal Naval logo.

"Well Karen, what do you think?" Wilson mused to his executive officer. "I know you had some personal plans for this weekend and I am imposing on you, lumbering you with the '*Boathouse*' whilst I'm away, but needs must."

The Boathouse was the local term of endearment used by the sailors and staff of the naval facility at Faslane to describe their workplace, one of the most strategically positioned and important naval bases in the country and the home of the UK's nuclear submarine fleet.

"Probably getting their knickers in a twist over nothing sir," Commander Duffy replied.

"But I suppose we have to go through the motions, to keep our politicians gainfully employed, and away from the booze and their mistresses," she added sarcastically.

"Yes Karen. I'll be damned if you are not right," he said with a grin. "But you never know. Let's get the big picture and we can take it from there."

"Will you be alright here while I'm away?" "Lorna knows all my current commitments and will help you out."

"Yep. No problem, sir. Go down there," she said, referring to his pending southward journey to the UK Capital, "and show them just how indispensable we are."

"I will certainly try Karen, and thank you."

"Let the log show that the Boathouse is now under your command!"

"Oh!" he added, realising he had a lot to do before he left. "Have Lorna call my wife please and let her know I won't be home and tell her I will call her when I can."

Forty-five minutes later, Commodore Grant Wilson was on board a Royal Navy AW101 Merlin Helicopter 'en route' to London and his meeting with the UK Prime Minister and others, for what he would later learn would be the most important intelligence briefing in the history of the human race.

Chapter 15

The building at number 70 Whitehall, in the City of Westminster, Central London is where the Cabinet Office Briefing Rooms (COBR) normally referred to as COBRA, are located and is a crisis management centre where the UK government meets to coordinate the actions of various government bodies and departments, in response to a national threat or crisis.

It was the evening of 4th February 2022 and Commodore Grant Wilson had just arrived at the COBRA office building, in the rear of a dark blue Jaguar XF Government vehicle, ahead of the crisis meeting to which he had been specially summoned to attend.

"Hmm," Grant muttered to himself, "no press pack yet. This really is 'hush hush', but for how long I wonder?"

Once inside the building he made straight for the executive washroom, primarily for a comfort stop and to freshen up, before proceeding to the COBRA office located deep in the basement of the facility. Still in full naval uniform, Grant arrived at the briefing room at 6.35pm where, apart from a few government aides coming and going, he found himself the first 'delegate' to arrive. As per normal security protocol he switched off his mobile telephone and placed it in a bag for safekeeping by the concierge before entering the room.

The Commodore was particularly hungry, having had nothing to eat or drink since his hastily consumed cappuccino earlier that morning, other than some water he had carried on to his flight. He helped himself to coffee and 'finger food' that had been laid out on a trolly towards the rear off the cabinet office and sitting at the main table alone, he used a neatly arranged notepad as an impromptu coaster in an attempt to keep his section of the table clean whilst he devoured his food.

Having consumed his makeshift meal, and in a quirk of his personality, he gathered all of his food crumbs into a neat pile on his notepad and flicked the whole stack onto the table, covering the two places opposite in a light coating of food debris. He would later deny all knowledge of the incident with feigned indignation, when the rightful occupants of those seats arrived.

The COBRA committee room itself had no windows and only one door which served as the entrance and exit, save for an emergency door at the opposite end of the room, which led to emergency survival quarters. The chamber contained a large rectangular shaped polished wooden table in the centre of the room, capable of seating five people down each short side and eight people down each long side. At one end of the room the wall was dominated by eight very large television monitors which were capable of a multitude of tasks delivering images, information and video links to the occupants of the room either singly or in a coordinated array. Spaced along the centre of the table at regular intervals were highly sensitive microphones which would convey the voices of the attendees, to whoever was at the other end of their video call. The chairperson and their deputy usually seated themselves in the centre of the five seats directly facing the screens.

Although the table could seat 26 delegates, it was rarely used to full capacity, as those sitting in the seats opposite the chairperson would effectively be sitting with their backs to the information screens, therefore these five seats were only occupied at times of dire need. Additionally, the room contained ample supplementary seating around the walls, where a departmental aid or secretary might sit, in order to be close to the official they were supporting.

As well as the standard security requirements of such a facility, the room was immune to electronic surveillance, was soundproof, bombproof and had its own independent air, power and water supplies. All communications emanating from this room were encrypted with the latest government anti espionage technology which could only be deciphered by a handful of receiving stations around the world, one of which was located in the headquarters of the CIA at Langley, Virginia, USA.

Tonight's meeting was being chaired by the UK Prime Minister, Constance Chapelton, and in attendance were the other five members of the Nuclear Deterrent and Security subcommittee (NDS), which included the UK Home and Foreign Secretaries, the Chancellor of the Exchequer and the secretaries for Defence, and Business & Energy, as well as representatives from all three branches of the British Armed Forces and of course the MI6 Chief of Secret Intelligence, currently a Ms Marcella Houston.

As each delegate entered the room, they acknowledged one and other before taking their seat at the table. The members of the NDS subcommittee sat at the long side of the table that would place them on the Prime Ministers right. Everyone else sat on the left side of the table and all delegates had a clear and unobstructed view of the screens.

The delegates who had sat opposite Grant Wilson wiped the crumbs from their side of the table onto the floor with a look of disgust but otherwise made no attempt to ascertain how they had got there.

At 6.50pm the Prime Minister entered the room with a brown file under her arm. She placed the file on the table at her seat then personally shook hands with each delegate, all of whom she knew personally at some level. She poured herself a cup of coffee from the buffet table and took her seat. At precisely 7.00pm she pressed a button and all eight screens working as one, came to life, effectively turning the wall into a huge television monitor.

At the other end of the meeting, in the CIA offices in Langley, it was 2pm in the afternoon. Present on the screen, and chairing the meeting stateside was the CIA Director of Intelligence, Alberto DeSouza. DeSouza had been in the top position of American intelligence for the last three of the CIA's 73-year history. The 56 year old was an ex United States Marine Core intelligence officer, who had worked his way to the top of the intelligence community. He was in his current role, partly attributable to his work in tracing and bringing to justice the terror groups responsible for the 9/11 attacks in September 2001, but mainly due to the fact that he was very good at what he did.

With DeSouza, sat the entire body of the Joint Chiefs of staff of the USA, indicating the importance of which the Americans placed on this intelligence, and the credence of the perceived threat it contained.

Constance Chapelton began the meeting by bidding the Americans a good afternoon and introducing herself and the entire room to their 'cousins' on the other side of the Atlantic. Alberto DeSouza did likewise for the American side. Pleasantries over the Prime Minister began.

"So, Mr DeSouza," Chapelton opened in her best business tone. "I believe you have some information on Bectel Incorporated that you wish to share with us?"

"I have had sight of a summary of what we are here to discuss, and thank you for that," she said holding up the folder she had brought to the meeting, "but for the benefit of everyone else, both here and 'stateside', I would be grateful if you could kindly bring us all up to speed."

"I do indeed, Madam Prime Minister," DeSouza retorted in his thick Louisiana accent, causing the British contingent to focus carefully on his narrative in an attempt to understand what was being said.

DeSouza went on to advise the group that Langley had been watching Harrison Becker, CEO of Bectel Incorporated, for some years and that they had recently 'plucked some intelligence out of the airwaves', meaning that they had intercepted some mobile communications data, relating to various construction projects that Bectel were involved in.

DeSouza went on. "This intel relates back to 2016, when Becker and his delegation were known to have met with the Chinese government over a three day period. We have been keeping a really close eye on him ever since."

"We believe," DeSouza continued, "that amongst other concerns, Bectel has been engaged by the Chinese to develop some sort of advanced propulsion system in relation to space travel. Probably a Trans Warp Drive or something similar, that will drastically reduce the traveling times of interstellar space flight. Our own scientists at NASA currently estimate that, with an appropriate space vehicle, an effective Trans Warp Propulsion System could cut the journey time to Mars to around six weeks, and to the Moon in a matter of hours."

"If the existence of this technology is confirmed, it would negate the need for a near Earth space docking and refuelling facility and effectively give the Chinese, and anyone they are prepared to 'get into bed with', implying that the Russian government was in on this too, a ten to fifteen year lead on our current technology." As he said the words *ten to fifteen years,* he spoke slowly and deliberately, to emphasise the ramifications for NATO if such a situation was permitted to become a reality.

"In short ladies and gentlemen, it means that Mars could effectively be colonised and controlled by the communists. A fitting metaphor for the celestial body commonly known as the Red Planet," he added sarcastically. Even allowing for the time differential, as the communication was encrypted and bounced around the globe, the silence in relation to this accusation was palpable and the humour, apparently lost.

DeSouza rallied and went on. "It is our understanding that these 200m high pyramids that are springing up around the world are attributable to Bectel, and are some sort of secret research and testing facilities. The common link here is that Bectel is involved in the construction of each one of the four structures we know of around the globe, and each one has come to be within a relatively short time period, coincidentally all within five years or so of Becker's meeting with the Chinese." "Now interestingly enough," DeSouza went on, interpreting his latest intelligence brief into the simplest language he thought appropriate, "none of these pyramids are anywhere near Russia or China and opinion is divided amongst our analysts as to why." "Perhaps plausible deniability," he mused adding, "If it isn't in their back yard, then maybe we will think that they have nothing to do with them."

"A more likely explanation however is that if something does go wrong, and one of these things goes boom, that boom is likely be catastrophic for those living in the immediate vicinity, but it will be sufficiently far away from the Chinese or the Russian homelands, that they will not have to worry about the fallout," adding to his narrative that his use of the word *fallout*, meant both in the political and the radioactive sense.

Proud of what US intelligence assets had uncovered he went on to add; "The four structures we know of are all complete, and in the hands of Bectel's Intelligence and Security Division. In addition, each one is effectively an impenetrable fortress, constructed of 5m thick reinforced concrete. We presently have no idea what is inside, although by the amount of what we believed to be a special liquid concrete mix that has been transported to each structure, we suspect that it may be shielding for some kind of nuclear fission that will be taking place inside."

"Now from what our satellite reconnaissance can tell us there are four of these structures around the world, but there may be more!" "If only four, then why?" "We don't know that yet either," indicating that his intelligence assets still had some work to do, "but we have our people on it now, and will get to the bottom of this shortly. Incidentally it is also under consideration that North Korea and perhaps India are in on this too, and although such an allegation fits with their national acquisition profiles, there is currently no credible intelligence to support this."

"It may be of course," he went on in his southern drawl, "that some of these structures are decoys, designed to confuse NATO resources in the case of an attack, meaning that the chances of destruction of the single pyramid, where the secret project was taking place, would in all probability be greatly reduced."

"The four pyramids we know of are located in Ecuador, Central Africa, Indonesia and a small island called Kiritimati in the republic of Kiribati, which is in the middle of the Pacific Ocean, south of Hawaii, the last location being thousands of kilometres from anywhere."

Coming to the end of his brief, DeSouza concluded, "If any of these structures are in fact decoys then we reason that the pyramid at Kiritimati, due to its remote location, is the one most likely to be the real thing, and it is at Kiritimati that we believe the secret research will be taking place, consequently it is there where we should concentrate our efforts." Apart from satellite images of the pyramids on a smaller 'screen within a screen' window while DeSouza had been speaking, the CIA chief's image had been dominating the screen. Now that he had finished speaking, the CIA camera zoomed out to include the whole of the American delegation.

"Thank you for that summary, Mr DeSouza," Connie Chapelton retorted. "May I assume your Joint Chiefs are in agreement of the assimilation of your recent intelligence?"

As one, the American Joint Chiefs nodded silently in agreement with their CIA colleague.

"Fine," she said. "Before we enter into any form of discussion, I will enlighten you to the British Intelligence perspective of the issue."

Turning to face her own staff, the PM nodded towards her Chief of Secret Intelligence and said; "Marcella, if you please," quietly resuming her seat. The PM had offered the floor to Marcella Houston and as she began to speak the camera zoomed in on her, filling the screen on the American side with her image. Like DeSouza, Marcella Houston was in post also because she was very good at what she did. She put her hand to her mouth, coughed lightly and began.

"MI6 has ascertained that there are indeed four, and only four of these structures." She was emphatic on this point.

"Viewed externally," she went on, "each pyramid is identical in every way."

"To be factually correct," she pronounced, "they should actually be termed 'tetrahedrons', which is the mathematical expression for a three-sided pyramid with no parallel faces, however referring to them as 'pyramids', trips off the tongue easier and is not an issue for us."

This was a subtle 'put down' aimed directly at the CIA intelligence assets, by the MI6 Chief, the implication being that, 'if you have intelligence to disseminate then check your facts and make sure they are correct'.

"Our listening stations around the world," she continued, "have intercepted communications in relation to Bectel from many sources, which when analysed reveals that they are indeed behind the construction of these pyramids and additionally, by careful analysis of these communications, we have ascertained that each one has a codename and a dedicated security team." At this point the screen array split, with half of the area being given over to satellite images and data that were now being projected to support the MI6 brief.

"The pyramids, if I may call them that," Marcella went on, rather naughtily highlighting her earlier jibe, "when viewed from above, look like a gigantic 'play' symbol, the sort of the symbol one would find on any electronic audio or video device."

"In fact, the structure in Africa, which is allegedly purporting to be a power station, has attracted the nickname the *'Play Station'* by the local population for this very reason."

"In Ecuador the structure is codenamed *Black Horse,"* she continued, "and is supposed to be some kind of 'state of the art' entertainment facility. Bectel were granted permission to construct in this 2018, following a huge deal to sponsor Antonio Varas's Ecuadorian government in their Education Reform Programme."

"In the DRC, in Central Africa, the pyramid, as I've just said known locally as the 'play station', has the codenamed *Red Horse* and professes to be a self-contained power plant, facilitating a new hospital complex being built to serve all of central Africa. That hospital complex is a humanitarian project, led by the new government there and is being funded by none other than Bectel, and for which Becker himself has been nominated for a Nobel Prize," she added, her tone ringing with incredulity.

"In Indonesia, in the west of Borneo near to the city of Pontianak, the pyramid has the codename *Pale Horse* and, like in Africa, is supposed to be a power station serving all of West Kalimantan, which is a huge geographical territory."

"This fact alone, if substantiated, would suggest that the power source within *Pale Horse* would have to be nuclear, as that is the only fuel that could generate enough power to satisfy the magnitude of the task it was designed to fulfil, and cleverly enough would account for any traces of nuclear fission activity, should any be detected at the site. The autonomous government arrangement in Indonesia provides scope for local officials to, well govern I suppose, and we suspect that a modicum of *'quid pro quo'* is how Bectel acquired the contract to build their pyramid there. It would appear that Bectel have convinced the Kalimantan government that their relatively small facility can supply sufficient energy to meet the growing needs of the wider economy, meaning a smaller environmental footprint hence the primary reason they may have been granted the contract."

Pausing only to check that the delegation was still following her, Houston continued.

"And finally, we come to *White Horse*, the codename assigned to the pyramid at Kiritimati in the Pacific." "The Kiritimati pyramid is supposed to be a gigantic 'pressure release valve', constructed to contain any potential geothermal activity that may be likely to occur due to the after effects of blast testing of nuclear bombs carried out on the island in the late 1950's and early 1960's."

Ms Houston purposely elected not to mention that the nuclear testing she was referring to, which exposed many allied service personnel to fatally high doses of radiation and caused untold devastation to the landscape, in what was otherwise considered to be an idyllic island paradise, was in fact carried out primarily by the British, and latterly the American governments, in their attempts to maintain supremacy over the then Soviet Union at the beginning of the cold war years.

"We are not yet certain why the structures have equestrian related codenames however Becker's former family home in Texas, which he still owns, is a fully functional horse breeding ranch and the consensus is that this may have some bearing on the nomenclature of the structures."

"MI6 also acknowledges that Kiritimati is very remote with the least risk of interference from third parties, being approximately two thousand miles south of Hawaii, in the middle of the Pacific Ocean, and if any of these structures is likely to be the testing ground for a secret propulsion system, then we agree with the CIA that it is likely to be Kiritimati."

Pausing for breath and a drink of water, Houston steamed on.

"As CIA intel correctly indicates, the pyramids are constructed of 5 metre thick, reinforced concrete. What we are not so sure of is if whether this design parameter is to keep external threats out, or internal exothermic activity in, and away from the 'all-seeing eyes' of our birds." Houston was referring to the spy satellites controlled by the British and American military, equipped with infra-red, ultra violet and radiation sensing technology and which are constantly circling the globe.

"In any case, we have determined that destroying the structures by any kind of conventional weapons strike is risky on two counts."

"Firstly, we don't know what is inside each pyramid and in the 'best case scenario', if only one of the pyramids is 'live', what kind of material it might contain." she was referring to the possibility of one of these structures being an actual development location for an advanced energy source adding, "The resulting explosion of unknown materials could be catastrophic, and of a magnitude so great that our current computer models have insufficient data to yet accurately calculate the devastation that would ensue," further adding "possibly leading to a worldwide catastrophe similar to the Chernobyl disaster in 1986, but on a much grander scale."

"And secondly, our scientists advise that the tetrahedron shape is the most efficient structure to withstand an airborne explosion, therefore to penetrate a reinforced concrete pyramid of five metre thickness, we would need a low altitude nuclear explosion of such magnitude that it would dwarf the bomb which destroyed Hiroshima in 1945, and devastate everything within a 30km radius of the site."

"Excuse me Prime Minister," Phillip Tercel, the UK Secretary for Business and Energy interposed, raising his finger to attract the PM's attention.

"I have some fresh information on that, which I only received this morning and which you may wish to consider before we go on."

Chapter 16

The Prime Minister motioned for Tercel to take the floor and as he began to speak the camera moved off the MI6 Chief, who was visibly annoyed at being interrupted, and on to Tercel automatically zooming in on him.

Nervously he began. "My department have only just come into possession of a case containing blueprint documents for the Bectel pyramid power facility in the DRC. The documents were handed over by a doctor administering medical aid in the DRC and were found by him in the middle of the Salong National Park in the DRC in Africa, on or around the 4th October 2020." "It is believed that these blueprints came from the wreckage of the aircraft carrying Benjamin Ngoy, a government official who was killed when his plane went down in that area on 25 September of that year."

Benjamin Ngoy, the man to which Tercel was now referring to was indeed a former DRC government ministers aid, with oversight of the building of the hospital and its power supply at Kisangani. Ngoy was previously considered a world expert in large scale construction projects involving reinforced concrete.

"My apologies for the delay in obtaining this information, however the reason it has taken so long to get our hands on these blueprints was that the doctor was on an extended tour of duty in the African Bush, and only handed these in to our embassy in DRC when his tour finished in late December 2020."

"The blueprints were subsequently logged and then stored at our Embassy in the DRC, only coming to light when an 'eagle-eyed' intelligence operative, based at the embassy, received an intelligence request in support of this meeting just a few days ago. Our Embassy in the DRC confirm that the case does indeed contain blueprints of the pyramid structure at Kisangani, and have forwarded us authenticated copies for examination."

"What of it?" the Foreign Secretary David Mallory rudely interrupted, the disdain in his voice palpable for anything that Tercel thought important. Continuing with his rebuke, Mallory continued. "The blueprints for these pyramids are a matter of public record and are available electronically to anyone who needs to view them," adding, "any teenager who knows his way around a computer could hack the government server and obtain a copy of the blueprints for us, for the price of a pizza and a four pack of light beer."

"Not these blueprints!" retorted Tercel angrily, annoyed at the interruption.

Tercel and Mallory had a history and did not get on at all, ever since Mallory beat Tercel to the Foreign Secretary post through his 'old pals act' and his Cambridge university connections. That was Tercel's opinion anyway, and the animosity that existed between the two was well known in cabinet circles. Happy that he was about to deliver a ministerial 'slap down' to Mallory in front of the PM, the Americans and the rest of the NSC, Tercel continued.

"These hard copy blueprints are thought to have been in the possession of Benjamin Ngoy on the day that he died, as they bear his office stamp and are different from those blueprints currently on file."

"And in what way are they different Mr Tercel?" enquired the Prime Minister, seeing past the animosity, "and is it significant to our current enquiry?"

"Yes Ma'am, I believe it is," Tercel replied confidently.

"The found blueprints are almost identical in every way to those readily available elsewhere, except that the blueprints Ngoy was carrying show a 'design flaw' in one of the sides of the DRC pyramid. The drawings clearly show that one of the faces of the DRC structure, the one that faces directly west, was constructed of half metre thick, partially reinforced concrete, and not five metre thick, fully reinforced concrete, like the other two faces."

Tercel was on a roll now and he could see that all eyes were on him. With a thought to the next cabinet reshuffle, he continued, his self-assurance increasing rapidly.

"This anomaly could be construed as a typo however it is common knowledge that someone of Ngoy's calibre would not tolerate such an error and would want to verify something like this personally. We believe that this was the reason why Ngoy made the trip to Kisangani on the day that he died, his intention being to inspect the Kisangani pyramid and confirm if this was indeed a typo. We conclude that it is highly possible his death was due to him discovering that this anomaly is in fact, correct."

"Are you suggesting Ngoy was murdered because he had stumbled upon a secret design flaw in one of these pyramids?" uttered the PM incredulously.

"It certainly looks that way Ma'am. Ngoy appears to have been murdered to silence him for what he had uncovered about the design of the Kisangani pyramid!"

The delegates on the US side of the screen began chattering at the implications of this new information, and those in the COBRA briefing room did likewise. Marcella Houston began scribbling furiously on her notepad whilst Wilson sat in deep contemplation, eyebrows raised at this revelation, and taking it all in.

All through the conference Wilson had been silent, scribbling on his notepad and awaiting the moment when he may be asked to render his opinion. Wilson had no reason or desire to impress those in the room, or those on the other side of the screen for that matter. His brain worked like a supercomputer and his reputation was well known throughout the intelligence community and every single seat at that meeting, on both sides of the Atlantic, knew of his accomplishments. The Intelligence revelation from Tercel certainly peaked Wilson's interest and he noted carefully the construction parameters and orientation of the DRC pyramid.

To the untrained eye, Wilson's notes would have looked like a collection of doodles, but to Wilson they meant a great deal. 'Summary and coding', was the formal name he gave to his unique system of note taking, but normally referred to it as 'sumcode'. Developed many years previously when he was at high school, he never disclosed its purpose to anyone, and kept its origin a closely guarded personal secret.

'Sumcode', was in fact the analytical tool partly behind the secret of Wilson's intellectual success and one which he would use to summarise and score packets of information, in real time, and as they came to his attention recording them in numerical, pictorial and diagrammatical form. He would allocate a particular element of a discussion a heading or title, and then take brief notes in the form of bullet points and pictorials, following which he would immediately assign a score to that part of the discussion in his own secret code of letters and numbers, all from parameters that he himself had devised. This provided him with an instant evaluation of what he was hearing, based on all of the relevant information he was receiving at the time, similar to the way that a secretary would take and later decipher notes written in shorthand. This allowed Wilson to empty his mind so that it was fully capable of analysing the next packet of information that came along, with maximum scrutiny and efficiency.

Gifted with an eidetic memory since childhood, Wilson would

have been able to recall every word and symbol on his notepad directly should the need arise, however being a lifelong fan of Homer Simpson, the head of the fictional Simpsons family, he would often joke with his wife Julia, quoting his cartoon idol who was known to have said;

"Every time I learn something new, something old drops out of the other side of my brain."

This was not true of course and this self-deprecating comparison, with the stupid clumsy cartoon father, was one that never failed to make Julia Wilson smile.

Always, at the end of any particular session or discussion, Wilson would briefly summarize all the packets of information that had been discussed and assign the whole document a master score, similar to his sumcode rating system, and it was on this score that he would base his further actions. Nevertheless, Wilson only stretched his brain when there was a specific need and his tried and trusted sumcode, which had never let him down throughout his entire academic life, was his way of ensuring this.

At the conclusion of Tercel's input to the meeting the PM nodded to Marcella Houston, who again took the floor, and with a forced polite smile, she continued.

"Now, getting back to Kiritimati," she went on, seamlessly picking up where she had left off. "We find ourselves presented with a paradox."

"A large-scale nuclear explosion, sufficiently large enough to fragment 5 metre thick reinforced concrete, would be less of an issue in the remote pacific, than any of the other three sites, where the magnitude of the loss of nearby human life and the resulting radioactive fallout would be wholly unacceptable. This fact alone raises the possibility, and here is the paradox, that if only one of these sites is a live development facility for an untested energy source, then perhaps we should consider the possibility that Kiritimati is *NOT* the most obvious location, and instead focus our attention on one of the other three sites, where the local population may be unwittingly acting as human shields, protecting the structure from such an attack."

"However," she was forced to acknowledge, "in light of the new intelligence brought to the table by Mr Tercel, I would concede that if correct, it would significantly reduce the amount of fire power required to breach any of these structures. Which I can now only speculate could perhaps be achieved by a conventional weapons strike, negating the need for a nuclear option." Finishing this section of her brief with, "All of which, unfortunately now leaves us none the wiser."

There was a bit of chatter amongst those on both sides of the video link at this revelation which the PM quickly quelled by standing and addressing the assembly.

"Order, order, ladies and gentlemen please," she called, the chatter quickly dying down and fading to silence. "Marcella, please go on," the PM added.

Houston got back into her stride. "Notwithstanding where we should focus our efforts and by what means we breach the structures, our analysis of the codenames given to each structure, lend weight to the China / Russia sponsored, Advanced Propulsion System theory."

"We have considered that *Red Horse*, the pyramid in Africa could be under Chinese direction. Similarly, *Black Horse* in Ecuador could be under Russian sponsorship. *Pale Horse* in Indonesia could be a veiled reference to a North Korean link, as they are moving to become a major global influence, and *White Horse* the Kiritimati pyramid, could be a very clever tactical decoy, as the resources required to deal with this remote location, as we have discussed, would be significant."

"Now then!" Marcella smiled gleefully, excited about introducing an alternative perspective to the discussion. "This may or may not be connected in any way, but back on the 1st October 2021, one of our satellite analysts picked up a house fire in western DRC, just north east of Kinshasa."

"A housefire in itself is not so remarkable," she conceded, "but what caught the analyst's attention was the intensity and the duration of this particular blaze, which initially burned with such ferocity that our autonomous satellite surveillance systems deemed it to be an ICBM missile launch and automatically initiated full UK defence protocols. This resulted in three British Typhoon fighters being scrambled out of Lagos in Nigeria, and a nuclear strike submarine in the South Atlantic being put on immediate alert. These assets were only stood down when human intervention confirmed the incident as a house fire."

Going into a little more detail of this incident Houston went on; "The property in question was a newly built colonial style mansion house belonging to Nava Tumeli, an African warlord and long-standing leader of the Congolese Freedom Fighters, known in the intelligence community as the CFF. Tumeli's property was just three weeks old and we suspect had been built with the proceeds of his extensive criminal empire, with all the latest building techniques, cutting edge materials and 'state of the art' fire suppression technology built in. Yet despite this the fire, in which Tumeli and his whole household perished, engulfed the entire property in less than a minute. It was initially thought this was due to there being either a munitions magazine or a fuel storage facility in the basement of the property, although strangely there were no reported additional explosions, as would normally be the case with random ordinance detonations."

As Marcella Houston paused for breath before continuing, Grant Wilson's attention again peaked at the mention of the intensity of the Tumeli fire, and he focussed intently on what was coming next.

"The cause of the fire remains unknown at present and the local fire chief was stumped as to the reason for the ferocity and intensity of the resulting inferno. Try as they did, the firefighters were unable to extinguish the blaze which continued in its ferocity, even when all the apparent fuel was consumed. The intensity of the blaze eventually ceased of its own accord after about 20 minutes or so, and the flames extinguished themselves shortly thereafter. Strangely enough, none of Tumeli's rivals are claiming responsibility for the act, but that might be something to do with the death of Tumeli's three wives and thirteen children and the backlash such negative publicity would have generated."

Now in the final stages of her brief, Houston had begun to wind down.

"All of the bodies except one, were completely consumed in the fire and very little remains of that, other than a torso and some remnants of charred clothing. That remaining body, which was found apparently attempting to shelter in an underground well, is at the mortuary in Kinshasa and the site had been secured until further investigation could be completed."

"That, ladies and gentlemen, is the most up to date intel MI6 have on the situation." Houston was bringing her intelligence segment to a close. "However, it is only prudent that we consider the additional information provided by Mr Tercel, in order that we can formulate and accurate and appropriate interpretation as to what it all adds up to."

Marcella concluded; "Prime Minister, ladies and gentlemen. That is my report which I submit for your consideration." The MI6 chief gathered her notes and, tapping them into a neat pile, sat purposefully back in her seat.

The PM openly thanked Houston and addressed the meeting for

the final time that evening.

"Ladies and gentlemen. It is now getting late here in the UK," the local time was just after 9.30 pm "and I suggest we take away what we have heard in this forum and discuss what it may mean."

"May I suggest we reconvene at the same time tomorrow where we can bring to the table our respective interpretations on what we have heard here this evening, on what we believe Bectel is up to and more importantly, what we collectively intend to do about it?"

With all in agreement, the video call was terminated. As the delegates rose to leave the room the Prime Minister called across the table.

"Marcella, Grant, could you both stay behind for a moment please? I would like a word."

Chapter 17

At the candid, and most definitely unofficial, 'after brief meeting' the PM had just called between Houston, Wilson and herself, all formalities were disregarded and plain speaking was the order of the day. As soon as they were alone in the COBRA office the Prime Minister began, firstly directing her attention to the MI6 security chief.

"Marcella!" she exclaimed, visibly irritated and her tone modified somewhat from the composed and professional business persona she had adopted during the previous meeting.

"What the fuck was that all about, sticking it to the CIA like that?"

"I get it that the screen was filled with a bunch of narcissistic, testosterone filled wankers, but fucking the Director of the CIA with that covert snyder of yours," she was referring to the MI6 chief's rude correction of the CIA Director on the mathematical inaccuracies of the pyramid structures, "and in front of the Joint Chiefs of Staff. What were you fucking thinking?"

The PM was building herself up towards a full-blown rant.

"Not that their intel was much fucking good anyway," she added. "We knew all that shit of theirs more than a month ago." "And as for intelligence?" she rasped. "It was like watching the fucking history channel."

"I'm sorry about that," Houston retorted sheepishly, referring to her less than professional attack on the CIA chief, "It won't happen again," she added apologetically.

"You're fucking right it won't!" Chapelton said with a decisive inflection in her tone, and just as her anger was beginning to subside, she turned her attention to Commodore Wilson.

"Grant. I need to know what the fuck is going on here." Her anger, escalating again, was being directed towards, but not at, the Naval Commodore in a desperate plea for answers.

"What the fuck is Harrison Becker up to? Is this propulsion system an achievable reality?" "Please, please tell me Grant," she said utterly exasperated, "that you have some idea what the fuck is actually going on here."

Fuck was a word that Constance Chapelton used a lot in private. The unladylike habit had begun in her rebellious teenage years, where it had perpetuated on through university and early adulthood and now it positively refused to desert her in her middle age. Although on this occasion her frustration was being vented here in private, she was often heard to insist that these frequent outbursts of hers, for which she was known to refer to as her 'personality quirk', were a mechanism by which she kept herself sane in the murky world of politics, and both of the individuals in the room knew that they were not the direct targets of her wrath.

In fact, and to the contrary, it was Chapelton herself who was directly responsible for the appointment of both Marcella Houston and Grant Wilson to their current postings, and secretly she had a soft spot for both.

"Grant," The PM now implored. "Please tell me you have something," her tone having softened somewhat.

"Ma'am as you know…" Wilson began, but his response was cut short.

"Cut the Ma'am shit, Grant! We are all alone here," she snapped, cutting him off obviously frustrated at the lack of answers. "As I've told you a hundred fucking times before, when we are in private its Connie!" that being how Constance Chapelton preferred to be addressed by her close friends and family. Duly chastised, Wilson continued;

"Connie," he began again cautiously. "From what I have just heard this evening, I have the beginnings of an initial theory about what may be actually going on here, but it is so 'out there' that I am worried that you would not believe me if I told you. So, I will have to check a few details before I advance my thoughts to you." Finishing with, "You are going to have to trust me on this."

"Trust you!" the Prime Minister came back, despondently. "Do I have a choice?"

"You know how I work Connie," Grants voice and demeanour also began to soften, "so no, I'm afraid you don't have a choice," he said emphatically. "You will have to trust me, or fire me," he added, knowing full well what course of action his friend would take.

"Marcella," Wilson said, turning to the MI6 chief in a distraction tactic, his smooth baritone voice bringing much needed calm to the situation.

"I'm going to need your help to check a few things." "Do you have assets in DRC at the moment?"

"Yes, of course," the intel chief replied.

"What about Ecuador?" Grant enquired.

"Yes, we have assets there too."

"And Indonesia?"

"No," she replied. "But depending on what you are after I could have someone trustworthy there by tomorrow morning."

"And Kiritimati?" Grant added.

"Fuck, no Grant. It's in the middle of the fucking Pacific Ocean. Other than an agent with a personality disorder and a coconut fetish, who in their right fucking mind would want to be stationed in Kiritimati?"

It was clear to Wilson that the PM and the MI6 chief seemed to have both attended the same finishing school.

"Ok, ok," Grant replied, trying to avert another excessive outburst from either of his two colleagues.

"I need one of your agents to get to the DRC as soon as possible and go to that Mortuary in Kinshasa."

"I want them to locate whoever carried out the autopsy on the remains of that body and I want an annotated copy of their report, as well as analysis of blood and clothing samples taken at the time. Additionally," he added, "I want fresh samples of internal lung tissue analysed, if there is anything left of them. And if it's not too much trouble, I also need soil sample analysis from the ground surrounding what's left of the foundations of the Tumeli house. Oh, and I need the results here with me by tomorrow lunchtime. Can this be done?"

"Of course," Marcella replied with a confidant air of certainty. She had the authority to wield the full intelligence resources of the British government and when it came to issues of national security, those resources were infinite.

"Do you have satellite images of all four pyramids, sorry tetrahedrons?" Grant asked, correcting himself in an attempt to diffuse a tense situation with humour. Getting the joke Connie Chapelton let out a muffled giggle.

"Yes," Marcella replied, placing her hands on her hips and casting an exasperated glance at Wilson. "We have detailed photographic analysis of all four sites."

"And you are sure that there are four, and only four of these pyramids?" Wilson enquired.

"Positive," Marcella confirmed, a scowl taking form across her face. "Were you even listening to my fucking brief?" "There are only four of these," she chose the word carefully, "structures around the globe, and they are in the locations that we specified during the briefing," a wry smile now displacing the scowl, acknowledging that she got the joke too.

"And each one is outwardly identical and not more than four years old?" Grant enquired.

"Yes, Yes, and Yes." "Where the fuck are we going with this Grant?" Marcella's voice rang out, beginning to rise in pitch.

"Where the fuck indeed?" interjected the Prime Minister, feeling the need to add her own tuppence worth to the conversation, in support of the MI6 chief.

"Well," said Grant. "If the other three have the same constructional parameters as the African blueprints suggest, a secret that an African government minister's aid died trying to expose, then I think I may have a very good idea of their intended purpose."

"All I can tell you both at the moment is that the pyramid structures are not designed to conceal an advanced propulsion system, prevent an eruption, nor house a Philharmonic Orchestra or a nuclear power generation facility."

The PM permitted herself a smile. She knew Wilson did not deal in guesswork and had seen him operate like this before. Grant was onto something and she trusted his instincts, knowing that he would tell her his thoughts as soon as he was certain.

"Marcella," she said, directing her gaze directly at the

intelligence chief. "Whatever he needs, I want you to make it happen," adding "and I want kept in the loop before", looking at each one in turn, "BEFORE," purposely repeating the word for greater emphasis, "we share this with the cousins."

"Understood," they both replied in unison, each nodding their understanding of the Prime Ministers private instructions, which they knew superseded anything she was likely to say in a public forum.

"Well let's get fucking on it then!" the Prime Minister concluded, taking each one by the arm and exiting the room.

Chapter 18

It was 9.45pm when Grant left the COBRA offices and having retrieved his mobile phone from the concierge, he stepped out into the cool evening air of Whitehall where his car was waiting.

"Where to sir, your hotel?" his driver asked politely.

"No," said Wilson, "change of plan." "I would like to go to Naval Admiralty HQ at Portsmouth please, and can you get me a coffee at a petrol station on the way."

"Yes sir, very good sir," his driver replied.

Wilson settled in for the two-hour car journey to navy HQ in Portsmouth, where his boss and former mentor, Admiral Sir Durnian Cruickshanks, would be eagerly awaiting his arrival. Wilson called the Admiral 'en route,' to let him know he was on his way.

Wilson's driver made good time to Portsmouth and it was 11.30pm when he reached the door of the Admirals quarters, located at the heart of the Naval base. The Commodore dismissed his driver with words of gratitude and an instruction to return and bear him to London the following morning.

Once within the Admiral's residence the two men greeted each other with a hug of genuine affection and when Grant had dumped his luggage in one of the three bedrooms of the Admirals home, and removed his uniform in favour of a pair of dark tartan lounge pants and a white T shirt, he made his way back to the lounge where his friend was waiting with a large crystal glass in his hand. Dressed appropriately for the time of day, The Admiral was wearing a burgundy robe over his dark silk pyjamas, complimented by a pair of black leather slippers.

"Scotch?" he asked his guest, already knowing the answer and provocatively waving a currently empty crystal glass in Wilson's direction. "I have a very nice Macallan 18 year old?" he proclaimed, as if there was a remote possibility that Wilson would refuse such an offer.

"You know fine well it's called Whisky sir, and a bloody good one at that. Scotch is what you southerners, and our cousins over the water call it," referring to the American generic term for Scottish Whisky adding, "and very few of them could truly appreciate such a fine liquid. But in answer to your question," he said, "yes, I'll have one, a large one please."

Sir Durnian Cruickshanks gave a deep belly laugh and poured his protégé a large glass of double cask, single malt whisky. It was indeed a Macallan 18 year old, an expensive indulgence and Wilson's favourite, and the fact that the most senior officer in the British Royal Navy knew that, spoke volumes of his fondness for the young man.

Sporting a large cigar in his hand the Admiral declared, "Doc says these will be the death of me," wafting the cigar in circles in front of his face. "Not allowed to light up you know, so I'm just going to suck on it old boy. Hope you don't mind."

"Not at all sir," Wilson replied, gratefully accepting his large whisky with the merest drop of water and just the way he liked it, which he immediately placed under his nose to appreciate the subtle and delicate aroma.

The two men made themselves comfortable and began to talk. For such an intimate setting the Admiral would normally insist on first name terms with his guest however having had this conversation with Wilson on numerous occasions, the young Commodore was adamant on referring to his mentor as 'sir', citing that he didn't have the mental capacity to switch between formal and informal interactions. Cruickshanks, who was fully familiar with Wilson's resume, found this self-depreciative assessment to be incredibly humorous and in this one regard alone, tolerated Commodore Wilson's blatant disregard of his orders.

It had just gone 11.50pm and as the logs banked high in the fireplace crackled comfortingly, the Admiral took a suck of his cigar and, exhaling loudly, sat back on the sofa.

"So, my boy," he said with the affection akin to that of a loving father. "What do you have for me?"

"Well sir," said Grant. "For starters, Mallory and Tercel are still at each other's throats." describing briefly the uncomfortable exchange between the Foreign Secretary and the Business and Energy Secretary, earlier in the evening.

"Marcella Houston rammed one up the 'tailpipe' of the CIA at the online conference this evening, and the PM is still suffering from severe Tourette's Syndrome." Wilson was referring to the PM's use of colourful language in the private meeting which took place after the official briefing. Cruickshanks laughed heartily at Wilson's informal summary of the evening's events.

"And what of the matter in hand?" The Admiral enquired, taking another suck at his cigar and turning to the serious business of the threat to national security.

"Your intel on that was spot on sir. Seems like the cousins," again referring to the universally accepted unofficial British term for the American intelligence services, "have got it right to be concerned about these structures popping up around the world."

"They are indeed connected to *Bectel Incorporated*, and Harrison Becker is definitely behind whatever it is they intend to do with them, but I don't think that intent involves developing an advanced propulsion system for space flight." "And." he added decisively, "I don't think the Chinese or the Russians are in on this either in fact, if I am reading this situation correctly, the purpose of these pyramids could be very sinister indeed, and for once the Chinese and the Russians are square in the firing line."

"I have to check a few details and MI6 are helping me with that but if I'm right, the whole of the Northern Hemisphere and a significant part of the south, is facing a global crisis and Bectel is most definitely at the centre of it."

"What I'm about to tell you sir is strictly speculation at the moment, and something I would never do with anyone else, so absolute discretion is required until I can confirm and report my findings to the PM."

Sir Durnian was familiar with the way in which Wilson operated, and consequently was acutely aware of the huge compliment his guest was just about to pay him. He took a sip of his whisky and with his inert cigar placed in the breast pocket of his pyjama's meantime, he sat back on the couch his ears open and his anticipation palpable.

Over the next hour or so, Wilson went on to convey his initial assessment of the impending crisis that the NATO nations were facing, and went on to give a comprehensive summary of his opinion, on what was actually going on.

Cruickshanks sat in silence, sipping on his Macallan, and feeling the need to periodically re employ his cigar. When Wilson had completed his speculative summary, he fell silent awaiting his

Boss's response.

"Good God man. Is what you are suggesting even possible?" he said, his gruff voice brimming with scepticism.

"Indeed, it is sir however, it is a scenario that is so 'out there', that I don't think it would even occur to the cousins, or anyone else for that matter, to contemplate it."

"And that's why we have you, my boy," the Admiral concluded with a loud 'ah ha', gulping the remainder of the amber liquid in his glass, and rising to provide himself and his guest with a refill.

"What about a time frame?" the Admiral enquired, standing with his back to his guest but maintaining eye contact via the antique mirror, which hung majestically on the wall adjacent to his drink's cabinet, pouring another two generous measures from the Macallan bottle as he spoke.

"Not Sure sir, but if my suspicions are correct, and if I was in Becker's position, I would be looking at a date in March this year, for practical reasons that would take too long to go into at the moment. I don't have the data to hand but when I do have it, I reckon I can pin it down to a window of a couple of hours around the third week in March, if my suspicions are correct."

"And if you *are* correct, what is the solution?" The Admiral added.

"Depends on what we are actually dealing with sir. Chemical analysis of that fire in the DRC should go some way to providing the answer to that."

"Good God man," the Admiral said again. "If this is what you suspect, Connie Chapelton will shit herself when you eventually get to brief her on your findings."

The night was getting old as the men ended their shop talk and wound the conversation down for the night with one more large helping from the whisky bottle, which by this time was now looking very sorry for itself.

"Time for me to turn in sir," Wilson stated. "I have a feeling that tomorrow is going to be a very long day."

"Goodnight, sir," Wilson said, as he made his way down the hall towards his bedroom.

"Goodnight m'boy," the Admiral retorted, remaining in his chair by the firelight and sucking hard on his unlit cigar, contemplating the ramifications of what he had just been told.

Chapter 19

The following morning, breakfast was served by the Admirals house staff at 7.00am precisely, marked by the ringing of a ships bell. The meal took place in the opulent dining room of the Admiral's Portsmouth residence, a room full of seafaring artifacts from throughout naval history, including paintings of some of the most famous officers, ships and battles that defined the British Royal Navy.

As Wilson entered the dining room he saw the Admiral, seemingly lost in thought, admiring a painting entitled, *'Twas in Trafalgar's Bay'*, a work by an unknown artist which seemed misplaced amongst some of the magnificent and rare masterpieces in the residence, but was one which pleased the Admiral. The painting depicted an ex Victorian sailor, now retired and dressed in a 'Chelsea Pensioner' uniform, and who had obviously been seriously injured during his service. The sailor was standing in front of a painting of the Battle of Trafalgar by JMW Turner, apparently using the work in an attempt to explain the intricacies of naval warfare to a young boy, himself an aspiring sailor, dressed as such in a late Victorian sailor suit. The Admiral considered the imagery in the painting which could well be himself, explaining naval tactics to Wilson, his young protégé and the nearest thing he had to a son, who one day he hoped would take his place, in service of his country.

Cruickshanks quickly snapped out of his reminiscence when his faithful servant Hamilton called the men to the table. As both sat down to a first course of porridge Wilson, having noticed the melancholy look on the Admiral's face, asked his mentor if everything was alright?

"Don't mind me," the Admiral replied solemnly. "Just a brief wave of nostalgia which has thankfully passed." "Now then," he said quickly changing the subject. "Tuck in to these rations' old boy. You have a very busy day ahead of you and you need sustenance," and with that both men ate and talked like old friends until the ships bell rang eight times. By eight fifteen Wilson was in a car speeding back to London, where he would seek to prove his hypothesis involving Bectel, and their true intentions.

By mid-morning, Wilson found himself ensconced in an office within the SIS building, which serves as the headquarters of MI6, and which is located near to where Vauxhall Bridge crosses the river Thames, in London. The office space, and the entire intelligence resources of MI6, had been placed at Wilson's disposal by his friend Marcella Houston, Chief of Secret Intelligence and on the direct instructions of the Prime Minister.

In the room was all available intelligence, satellite images and local asset information alluded to by Marcella Houston at the COBRA meeting the previous evening, and Grant Wilson devoured every piece of it, testing and retesting the validity of his hypothesis. By early afternoon the analysis of the items and data from the Tumeli fire in DRC, transferred overnight to MI6, had been acquired and was now being disseminated by the man on whom the UK government had selected to steer them through this crisis.

Still keeping his thoughts to himself, Grant Wilson was heartened that what he had learned so far supported his conclusions. He was due to meet the PM at 5.30pm that evening, at her home behind the famous black painted door of number 10 Downing Street in London, the UK Prime Ministers official residence, to update her personally on his conclusions before they attended the scheduled intelligence briefing with the Americans, planned for later that evening.

It was approaching late afternoon when quite unexpectedly, Marcella Houston knocked on the door of room B12, the Naval Commodores temporary intelligence 'compendium'.

"Got some new intel for you......and a cappuccino. Interested?" Marcella teased, stepping out from behind the half open door and waving in the air a carton, containing two drinks cups.

"Yes, to both." Grant replied, realising that he had consumed nothing but water since his breakfast with the Admiral.

As he sipped gratefully at his drink and the accompanying undeclared jam doughnut, Marcella, almost singing said, "I've been busy too-hoo," as she logged onto a computer terminal in the office and brought up the image of a man on the screen, along with an entire summary of the intelligence currently held on the individual.

As Houston and Wilson were the only occupants of the room, there was no need to observe normal secrecy protocols. Excitedly Marcella began by clicking through images of varying quality, of the individual in question.

"Does this man's picture ring any bells?" she said, her eyes bright with anticipation. Wilson's semi vacant look suggested that the answer to the question posed to him was, 'No.'

"I thought not," she said. "And now for the interesting bit." Clicking into the sub text attached to the images, and using the information to supplement her narrative, she began.

"We find ourselves at Kisangani Airport, on 25 September 2020, which is the date of Benjamin Ngoy's return flight to Kinshasa, and the last time he was seen alive. These are taken from CCTV images at the airport."

Grant sat and stared at her blankly, his drink in one hand and his partially eaten doughnut in the other, and shrugged his shoulders.

Still referring to the screen she went on; "The man in the image goes by the alias of Pierre Dubreton, whom we cannot yet positively identify. He is obviously in disguise and on this occasion he is purporting to be a government official, investigating smugglers trafficking drugs into and out of the DRC using light aircraft. Mr Dubreton here," she said stabbing the image on the screen with her finger, "interviews the pilot of a light aircraft shortly after he lands, and then has time alone searching his plane for contraband. Apparently, none was found." "We suspect Mr Dubreton may have planted some sort of device to disable the aircraft mid-flight because as you know, something brought the plane down in the middle of nowhere, making it look like pilot fatigue. The end result of this incident, being the death of Benjamin Ngoy."

"Any of this sound familiar?" she asked. "Let me give you a little clue. Bectel Inc."

His mouth temporarily empty, Wilson replied, "The Architect that was questioning the blueprints of the pyramids, sorry, tetrahedrons." he added, correcting himself.

"Ha ha, very funny, I don't think," Marcella retorted. She was on a roll now and continued.

"Ecuador, South America, 29 June 2021," she spoke, excitedly. "Bectel are constructing their pyramid near the capital Quito." She emphasised the word *pyramid* to indicate that this is how she would be referring to the structure from now on, reinforcing her words with a feigned cold stare at her guest. "Constructing their pyramid," she repeated, picking up where she had left off, "just west of Quito, having been given permission by the

Varas government to do so, as part of the deal for funding *Nueva Herencia's* Education Reform Programme."

"Remember?" she said. "I told you all this yesterday."

She carried on regardless. "Construction of the *Black Horse* pyramid had stalled due to labour and material supply issues, as the local drug cartels were disrupting the supply lines and executing local workers for what were minor infractions of their code. Information on this incident is scant as fear is preventing the locals from talking, however it appears that in an attempt to resolve the supply issue, this same individual again in disguise and under a different assumed name and persona, had a meeting with Santiago Torres, also known as *La Serpiente*, by far the most ruthless and influential of all the drug leaders in Ecuador."

"We believe that the only way this man would have got close to the Serpent was to make believe that the meeting was to enable the delivery of a financial tribute, probably in an attempt to bribe the Serpent to allow the project to get back on track."

"Anyway, the following day, the Serpents head shows up in a box at the offices of 'El Mundo', a local newspaper, creating a power vacuum and sparking a prolonged turf war with all the other rival drug factions in Ecuador, fighting for supremacy. Follow up investigations at the Serpents lair, revealed his decapitated remains and his entire personal bodyguard, all dead. Throats slit wide open! Post Mortem results revealed that they were likely unconscious when they were cut, bleeding to death on the floor where they fell."

"Connection? Bectel Inc!"

Rapidly approaching the conclusion of this piece of the puzzle, Marcella took a deep breath and summarised.

"Both Ngoy and the Serpent, threatened whatever Becker has planned for these pyramids, and both were eliminated for doing so. It is my considered opinion that this, as yet unidentified individual, is an assassin in the employ of Bectel and is effectively an 'in house problem solver', with the sole purpose of addressing issues which compromise the timely construction of these pyramids, which would explain why he has suddenly popped up on the grid at these times, and then vanished."

"And Tumeli?" Wilson asked inquisitively.

"There is no information at present of this man's involvement in the Tumeli killings but Tumeli, like the Serpent, had previously threatened the supply chain to the Kisangani pyramid and then suddenly and out of the blue, he and all of his family are incinerated."

"How did that happen?" "And if our man didn't do it, who did? Either way, I suspect it was only a matter of time."

"Whatever Bectel are up to, and whatever time line they are following, it's getting close. I can feel it, Grant." Marcella added, giving the distinct impression that she was heeding her instincts.

She looked expectantly at Wilson for some sort of validation of her findings, and as he had succeeded in the consumption of his doughnut, he wiped the last traces of sugar from his lips, took a sip of his drink, and began.

"Nava Tumeli," Wilson had an air of certainty as he spoke, "died from nothing more than greed and stupidity. Furthermore, I would be very surprised if your mystery assassin had anything to do with it, although I do agree that Tumeli was probably on this guy's 'to do' list."

"As regards Ngoy and the Serpent, I agree with you there. They were assassinated for compromising Bectel's carefully laid out plans. I reasoned that they had been 'eliminated', but I must confess I did not know by whom, but knowing what we know now, your intel makes perfect sense." This was not the resounding 'well done Marcella' she had hoped for, but Wilson's comments nevertheless drew a small smile of satisfaction from the MI6 chief.

Wafting his sumcode pad in the air as the font of all knowledge, which contained his notes from the previous evening and a summary of his conclusions that day, he spoke with a definitive air of authority.

"I know what Becker has planned, I know why he has planned it, and I now know when he is going to execute those plans."

"The only thing I do not yet know is how to stop him."

It was now 5.00pm when Grant Wilson, turning to his good friend said, "Marcella. I'm meeting the Prime Minister at 5.30pm, to update her before this goes across the Atlantic. Can you be at that meeting?"

"Try and stop me," she replied emphatically.

Thirty minutes later, within 10 Downing Street, Connie Chapelton, the UK Prime Minister met with her good friends Marcella Houston and Grant Wilson. The meeting was in her private accommodation in an attempt to keep it 'off the radar', and was intended to give the PM the heads up, prior to the official COBRA response at 7.00pm UK time later that evening, where all further facts would be established and discussed.

As well as being the British Premier, Connie Chapelton was also a mother and knew how to look after her guests. She rightly surmised that Wilson would have been hard at it, analysing all the material that Marcella would have provided, and would have not thought to stop and eat.

"I've made a pot of my signature chilli for you Grant, so we can eat while we talk, as I bet you have had nothing since breakfast."

As she plated the food into bowls, accompanied by basmati rice and garlic bread, she casually remarked to Grant, "By the way, will you be going back to Portsmouth after tonight's meeting?" subtly indicating that she was aware he had spent the previous evening in the company of his mentor, Admiral Cruickshanks.

"No Ma'am... I mean Connie," he replied, correcting himself before the swearing started.

"I've had nothing but a cappuccino and a doughnut since breakfast and in answer to your question," and pausing briefly for breath he said, "after what I have to tell you, if we are permitted to sleep, then for me it will be at the Chesterfield in Mayfair." the Chesterfield being Grant's preferred London Hotel.

As Grant eagerly munched through a bowl of chilli, washed down with sparkling water, he began his assessment of the situation to the two women. Both of his colleagues had pieces of information and intelligence relating to the crisis but neither had the analytical skills to extrapolate the data into what they both were being briefed on right now, by the man who was considered by many to be the world's leading expert in tactical and strategic defence operations.

Both women sat open mouthed and in silence, save the odd question to clarify the details of what they were being told, the consumption of food now the furthest thought from either of their minds.

"Grant!" the Prime Minister said, only barely believing what she had just heard, and only then because of the reputation of the man who had said it to her. "Is this even fucking possible?" If the mood had been lighter, Grant would have made a joke about the PM's 'Tourette's' kicking in again.

"I'm afraid it is Connie and we have, by my calculations, 43 days to find out how to prevent it from happening."

"And you are sure...," the PM was incredulous, "that neither the Chinese or the Russians are behind this?"

"Quite sure," Wilson replied. "In fact, by my reckoning both the Chinese and the Russians are going to be suffer most, if this scenario ever comes to fruition."

Connie Chapelton picked up a telephone in her apartment and dialled a six digit number, which was a coded hotline to CIA headquarters in Langley, Virginia, USA. Speaking in a solemn business tone she said, "Get me CIA Director DeSouza please, priority five call."

Moments later the recipient answered the call.

"Hello Connie, not cancelling our meeting, are you?" he said with light humour in his tone. "We are all good to go here, and just having some refreshments while we wait."

"No, I am not cancelling Alfonso," was the PM's succinct reply, "but if I was you, I would sit down. You need to hear this!"

Chapter 20

It was 7.15pm UK time, Saturday 5 February 2022, when the Prime Minister, flanked by her intelligence chief and top naval warfare strategist, walked purposefully into the COBRA briefing room. She apologised to all present for being uncharacteristically late, and activating the secure link which connected the room to her colleagues on the American side, she likewise apologised to them.

With no time to lose Connie Chapelton, perspiring lightly, began;

"Ladies and gentlemen. Having analysed the Bectel situation, and all associated intelligence currently available to us, we can state with near absolute certainty that we now know what Bectel is planning to achieve. We have a lot to get through this evening so if I may, I will pass you over to Commodore Grant Wilson of our Royal Navy, who will lead this evening's discussion and I suggest you listen very carefully to what he has to say."

"Commodore," she said, with an ominous look towards the officer, and motioned for him to begin.

Wilson's image was now projected into CIA headquarters where, as in the COBRA room in London, all eyes were on him. Wilson was dressed in his full Naval uniform, the cuffs of his blazer bearing the rank insignia that he had worked so hard to achieve and which was an endless source of pride for his family, in particular his mother Madelaine.

"Thank you, Prime Minister," Wilson began, standing to address the assembled company which this evening included some of the greatest military and analytical minds on the planet and who collectively were about to scrutinise everything he was about to say, and they would expect immediate and definitive answers. His stance, demeanour and tone all exuded the confidence of a man who was sure of himself and tonight of all nights he would have to be as the cynical minds, both in the room in front of him and across the Atlantic, would not be easily swayed.

In his hand he held a small device that would advance the presentation slides he was about to narrate. This included animations, photographs and live time video feeds, all of which were carefully chosen to assist him impart the complex intelligence narrative he had composed to accomplish the task of convincing the leaders of the western world that life as they know it was about to change.

"Good evening, ladies and gentlemen," he began, echoing the Prime Ministers polite greeting to the assembled company.

"Since we last spoke within this forum, a little over twenty four hours ago, intelligence has been streaming between us, all of which in one way or another, is related to the current threat we now face."

"Before I begin, I would like to pay tribute to the intelligence resources of our respective nations, men and women of both MI6 and the CIA, for bringing this information to us, often at significant personal cost to themselves and their families."

This sentiment drew a nod of approval from both Marcella Houston and her opposite number in the CIA, as well as positive mutterings from around both tables.

"I have analysed every bite of information currently available to me and in summary, I conclude that the threat posed by Bectel Inc. is real and imminent, but it is not what we first thought." Adding sombrely, "it is much, much worse."

There was the raising of eyebrows at this opening gambit, and further mumbling around both tables which quickly subsided, after which the silence awaiting Grant's conclusions was palpable as Wilson, by reputation, was not a man prone to exaggeration.

"First of all," he began in an assertive tone, "I can confirm there are indeed four, and only four of these pyramid structures around the globe."

"To be precise they are indeed tetrahedrons which, as we learned yesterday, is the correct mathematical expression for a three-sided pyramid with no parallel faces, but as previously agreed and for ease of reference, I will also refer to them simply as 'pyramids." He briefly made eye contact with Marcella Houston at this point however the gravity of what he was about to unleash on the assembled company, information passed to her approximately one hour earlier, robbed her of the chance to see irony or humour in the reference.

"Also, I will hereafter and in the name of simplicity refer to *Bectel Incorporated,* the company at the centre of our concerns founded and controlled by Harrison Becker, simply as 'Bectel'." Returning to the commencement of his brief he carried on.

"Bectel have assigned codenames to each of the four structures." This was no great surprise to the company as only the day before, everyone in the room had been made aware of the existence, but not the significance, of the code names.

"The four pyramids, as you know, have been identified as *White Horse, Black Horse, Red Horse and Pale Horse* respectively."

"Early intelligence reports suggested that the colour reference may be linked to a particular group or nation with an interest in that particular structure, for example Red Horse was thought to be attributed to or sponsored by the Chinese; Black Horse, the Russians; White Horse, the North Koreans and Pale Horse, tenuously linked to aggressive fractions within the Indian sub-continent."

"The prevailing thought was that each, or all of these groups, would have an interest in populating the Moon and Mars in an attempt to exploit the resources that exist there, and thus gain an advantage over the progressive western NATO countries, such as ourselves. And by implication, one or more of these groups were thought to be involved in a deal with Bectel that would deliver to them, advanced space technology, that would enable them to do so." Wilson was referring to the rumoured Trans Warp Drive System that Bectel had allegedly been secretly developing.

"This has since been found to be inaccurate," he said emphatically.

"There has been a disinformation regime at work, cunningly weaving false intelligence into what our people have been gathering and has had our assets chasing shadows all over the globe, resulting in us effectively taking our 'eye off the ball' so to speak, needlessly diverting our resources away from the real matter at hand."

The silence in both rooms was now profound, waiting for Wilson to continue.

"The colour references assigned to each of the four pyramids by Bectel actually, and rather ironically, allude to the 'Four Horsemen of the Apocalypse', referencing the punishments of God, as contained in the book of Zechariah in the Holy Bible, and more importantly what these punishments represent." As he spoke, an image appeared on the screen of an oil painting of the Four Horsemen of the Apocalypse, an interpretation by the artist Viktor Vasnetsov.

Vasnetsov's original work, currently housed in the Glinka State Central Museum of Music and Culture in Moscow, was painted in 1887 and depicts the punishments of God as described in the Old Testament of the Holy Bible.

The Four Horsemen of the Apocalypse by Viktor Vasnetsov, 1887

Describing the work Wilson continued; "The Painting shows four figures mounted on horseback, each one following the other, the first being a white horse representing conquest, then a red horse representing war, followed by a black horse representing famine and finally a pale horse, being ridden by a skeletal figure carrying a scythe, representing death."

Having narrated the details of the painting to the company, Wilson then added;

"This is an apt and, as it transpires, a highly accurate metaphor of what we are facing, which you can judge for yourself by the information I am now about to impart to you."

Wilson continued. "The pyramid in Kiritimati in the Pacific Ocean, has been codenamed *White Horse* by Bectel and, due to its remote location, experienced very little in the way of construction delays or issues. It was completed and became fully operational in October 2021. It is now under the strict control of Bectel's Intelligence and Security Division."

"*White Horse* is supposed to be, for want of a better analogy, an oversized pressure relief valve, built over a weakness in the Earth's crust, along a section of the geological area of intense volcanic activity, commonly referred to by geologists as the Pacific 'Ring of Fire'." "We have been led to believe that the purpose of *White Horse* is to contain an unforeseen and sudden volcanic eruption, sufficiently long enough to be able to evacuate the resident population to a place of safety. Bectel secured the commission to design and build the structure on the recommendation of the USGS and the UN, a structure which, due to its remote location, was deemed beyond the logistical and financial resources of just about any other company in the world."

"*White Horse* Stands 200m tall and in order to perform its supposedly intended function, it is constructed of 5 metre thick, reinforced concrete. What it contains inside, until recently, we did not know for certain." The phrase '*until recently*' served only to whet the appetites of the attendees, as it suggested previously unknown information regarding the contents of the pyramid would soon be forthcoming.

"When viewed from the air," Wilson went on, "*White Horse* is orientated in such a way that one of its three sides, faces exactly due west. This aspect of the structure will become important later in the brief," he added.

"This particular pyramid, mainly due to its remote location, had been identified by our intelligence sources as a potential site for the development of a new space propulsion system, known as Trans Warp Drive, which Bectel are supposed to be secretly developing in conjunction with the Chinese and the Russians. Although Trans Warp Drive, technically referred to as the *Trans Warp Propulsion System* (TWPS) is in theory possible, the link to the Chinese is false information and is the consequence of a cleverly weaved counter intelligence plot, carefully laid out for us to discover, giving credence to the story the belief in which masks the true purpose of the *White Horse* structure."

"Which is what? interrupted the UK Foreign Secretary David Mallory, breaking the silence.

"I'll get to that sir," Grant responded, looking for approval of his actions from the Prime Minister which she indicated by a nod of her head, casting her eyes downward in dismay.

Wilson went on. "Moving eastwards around the globe, we come to South America and the pyramid in Ecuador, which has the codename *Black Horse* and which was completed around late October 2021. Like the *White Horse* Pyramid, the Ecuadorian structure stands 200m tall and is constructed of 5m thick reinforced Concrete."

"*Black Horse* is supposed to be a 'state of the art' auditorium constructed to facilitate pop concerts, classical music festivals, exhibitions and the like, and Bectel were granted permission to erect the structure as a condition of their 15 billion dollar investment towards the Ecuadorian governments education reform programme. Although much less remote than the Kiritimati structure, *Black Horse* did experience completion issues due to interruptions in the supply of materials and labour. At the end of June 2021, these problems were resolved when the reigning drug lord in the region, known locally as *La Serpiente,* and his entire bodyguard were assassinated creating a power vacuum. *La Serpiente* was thought to be behind acts of coercion and disruptive activity in relation to *Black Horse*, seriously hampering its expeditious completion."

"We are now certain that *La Serpiente* was eliminated by an agent acting on behalf of Bectel, specifically because of his disruptive activities which were causing delays to the timely completion of *Black Horse*, which is now finalised and under the control of Bectel's Intelligence and Security Division until its 'official' opening."

"Like *White Horse* in Kiritimati, *Black Horse* is also constructed in such a manner that one of its three sides, faces exactly due west."

Wilson scanned the room and the monitors to see if anyone was 'getting it' yet.

"Coincidence? I think not. Let me continue." Like an experienced storyteller Wilson had captivated his audience and was now reeling them in.

"Continuing on our journey eastwards around the globe, we come to the pyramid in central Africa, in fact it is just north of the town of Kisangani in the Democratic Republic of the Congo, known of course to the rest of the world as the

DRC. Like its other two 'sisters', this structure stands 200m tall, it is constructed of 5m thick reinforced concrete and has the codename *Red Horse.*"

"This particular structure purports to be a 'state of the art' power generation facility which will provide nuclear power to most of the north of the DRC, including the new 'All Nations' Hospital facility, currently under construction just a few miles away." "Unlike the hospital which it will support, which is experiencing construction delays attributable to the worldwide Covid-19 pandemic, the *Red Horse* structure is fully complete and under the control of, none other than Bectel's Intelligence and Security Division."

"Intriguingly with *Red Horse,* an African Architect, himself a world expert in construction processes involving reinforced concrete, was assassinated because of his discovery that one side of the *Red Horse* structure is constructed of lightly reinforced concrete, a mere half metre thick, unlike the other sides which are five metres thick and fully reinforced. That Architect, as we heard yesterday, was Benjamin Ngoy and we are certain he was killed for exercising due diligence in his field of expertise, in what we strongly suspect to be a pre-arranged light aircraft crash approximately 17 months ago."

"Blueprints recovered from near to the crash site, later verified as those Ngoy was working on and brought to our attention by Mr Tercel yesterday, confirm that the weak side of that structure faces exactly due west."

"Now," said Wilson, briefly recapping. "Two such structures oriented as they are, could be a coincidence, but three?"

Again, before Wilson continued, he made a quick scan of the delegates which revealed a few raised eyebrows but nothing remotely resembling full comprehension of the facts yet. Instead, the entire meeting sat in expectant silence, transfixed on

Wilson, awaiting his conclusions.

"Then we come to the last of the group. The pyramid in Indonesia and the one we know least about. It has the codename *Pale Horse* and is located just north of the city of Pontianak, in the West Kalimantan region of Borneo. Like the structure in the DRC, it is supposed to be a power generation facility, ready after trials to provide power to all of West Kalimantan, a huge area which is undergoing rapid economic expansion. In order to satisfy the needs of that region and generate the colossal power output required, the facility would have to be nuclear in design, which is coincidentally exactly what we have been led to believe."

"Otherwise, the *Pale Horse* pyramid is identical in every way to the other three structures. We know very little else about *Pale Horse* other than the fact that its new owners are keen to get hold of it and get it online as quickly as possible. The West Kalimantan government have been given a completion date by Bectel of 20th March 2022, when the structure will 'go live' and start producing power. *Pale Horse* also, is fully completed and currently under the tight control of Bectel's Intelligence and Security Division until that time."

"And!" Wilson said, adding a touch of drama to the proceedings with what could be perceived as an unimportant afterthought, "did I mention that *Pale Horse* also has a side that is orientated exactly due west?"

At the conclusion of the information on the four structures, some spontaneous mumbling broke out among those present, and there was speculation as to what the significance of the western orientated face could mean, but essentially no one had grasped the full implications of the brief as yet.

Trying to continue with his momentum, Wilson announced, "If I could ask you to be patient, please. This will all come together shortly.   Ma'am, may I continue?" he asked again, looking across at the PM.

"Alberto," the Prime Minister enquired, directing her gaze at the CIA chief on the screen. "Any questions at this stage?"

"Please continue," DeSouza responded, having had the concise version of the brief by telephone from the British Prime Minister earlier, and anxious to hear the full unabridged explanation.

Grant Wilson took a long drink from a bottle of water sitting on the table beside his sumcode notes then, taking a deep breath, he went on with his brief trying to keep everyone with him.

"So far," he said, taking the opportunity to recap, "we have four pyramids around the globe, each one constructed in exactly the same fashion, each one with a side that orientates exactly due west, and thanks to Mr Ngoy, we know that the western face of the African pyramid is thinner and more fragile than the other two faces, which is almost certainly the case with the other three structures."

"Our most accurate presumption of the reason for this anomaly is that the western face of each pyramid is designed to implode or fail at a preselected time, exposing whatever is inside to the atmosphere."

"Are we looking at a bio-weapon?" General Mitchell Conroy, American Chief of Army asked.

"No sir," Wilson replied confidently. "Good question but highly unlikely, and I will tell you why."

"Firstly, the time and effort required to design and create such a large structure to house a bio-weapon does not make sense. Why build a structure, 200m tall and costing hundreds of millions of dollars, to house a lethal gas or liquid that could be contained in a tank the size of a gas truck? No, I think not," Wilson stated conclusively. "Such an excess would only attract unwanted attention and compromise the secrecy surrounding these structures, a secrecy that Bectel have been trying so diligently to maintain."

"Perhaps a fuller explanation will be forthcoming when we look at the location of each structure?"

"Each pyramid," he pointed out, "is either constructed on, or is very close to the Earth's equator. This fact has a significant bearing on its true purpose."

"In addition," he said before anyone could interrupt with a question, pressing a button on the device he was holding and employing computer graphics to assist him, "starting with the *White Horse* structure at Kiritimati in the Pacific Ocean and going east along the equator, we come to the *Black Horse* pyramid in Ecuador, approximately 10,000km away."

"Continue eastwards, still on the equator, and almost exactly 10,000 km later we come to the DRC and what do we have there? The *Red Horse* pyramid at Kisangani."

"Take our last step eastwards, still along the equator and in another 10,000km we come to West Kalimantan on the Island of Borneo, and more importantly the *Pale Horse* pyramid at Pontianak, located almost exactly on the equator."

"Now ladies and gentlemen," Wilson prepared himself, building anticipation as he advanced towards the conclusion of this section of his brief. "Factor into this equation that we know the circumference of the Earth at the equator is approximately 40,000km, you will see that these structures are positioned equidistant around the globe, that is one every 10,000km."

"Add to this circumstance that each structure has a west facing side, designed to implode at a pre-determined moment in time, then it is not so far a step to speculate that these structures are not volcanic eruption regulators, entertainment venues or power stations as they proport to be, and there is almost certainly no trans warp drive research going on inside any of them."

"I conclude, ladies and gentlemen, and now inform you with a very high degree of certainty that these pyramids are, for want of a better description, gigantic rocket motors, designed to operate in synchronicity, releasing unbelievable amounts of energy for a single purpose."

Wilson looked across to his Prime Minister for tacit permission to impart to the assembled company, the one sentence that would define his horrifying conclusions, the same conclusions he had relayed to her earlier that evening.

Receiving no body language to the contrary from the PM, who's features were pale and troubled, Grant Wilson took a deep breath and delivered his conclusions, and the essence of the subject of his analysis.

In a clear and confident tone, he announced;

"Harrison Becker intends to speed up the rotation of the Earth, and in doing so will plunge the whole world into a new ice age."

Chapter 21

There was a moment of silence around both sides of the video conference, suddenly shattered by an avalanche of statements and questions, the answers to which were necessary to allow the attendees of the meeting to absorb and assimilate what they had just been told. There followed a period of unintelligible chaos, where everyone seemed to be talking at once, when Constance Chapelton eventually intervened, calling the meeting to order.

As the melee began to diminish, Connie Chapelton called out; "Ladies and gentlemen please! I'm sure we all want to know the why, the how and the when, and it will be forthcoming if I could just ask you to bear with us."

It took a few moments for the clamour to subside but when it did, order was restored and Grant Wilson continued with his address.

"Thank you, Prime Minister."

"Around six or so years ago, as the CIA informed us yesterday, Harrison Becker had a secret meeting with the Chinese, a meeting that we were supposed to believe was regarding trade and commerce however we now know this was a front for another purpose."

"Becker, a staunch ecological champion and 'friend of the earth', was back then and currently still is, concerned about the phenomenon known as global warming, a phrase which I am sure we are all now familiar with. To be fair, Becker considered the phenomenon a credible threat to the planet long before it became a popular political football."

"Becker viewed the Chinese, with their ever-expanding population and insatiable desire for economic development, as the main contributors to the phenomenon, although it must be said Becker also holds the developed economies, and by that I mean us, responsible if albeit to a lesser extent."

"Becker tried to persuade the Chinese to reduce their carbon emissions at this meeting and long before it became the 'in' thing to do, probably offering assistance with the development of an advanced space propulsion system that we suspect his company had been working on, which was in fact the TWPS. The Chinese however, in their arrogance, believing they were near to finding a solution to Trans Warp Propulsion themselves refused and continued expanding as before, disregarding Becker's offer and more importantly his concerns for the planet. Becker, no doubt unaccustomed to being refused and probably incensed at the arrogance of the Chinese leadership, thereafter switched the sole focus of his company to the reduction of global emissions by way of the development of the four pyramids and of their purpose."

"A project we have since discovered he has named *Chrysalis*."

"When ignited, the four pyramids working in synchronicity will act like the outlets of a gigantic 'Catherine wheel', increasing the rate of the Earth's rotation about its axis, or in simple terms speeding up the Earth's rotation, shortening the length of a standard day, from the current twenty-four hours, to something less."

"But how will this result in an ice age and how is it possible?" the Home Secretary, Angelina Downs-Thornton asked from within the COBRA room.

"Without going into a natural history lesson Ma'am," Wilson replied, "it would work like this." Again, employing appropriate graphics to assist, Wilson soldiered on.

"The Earth, as you know, spins on its own axis completing one revolution approximately every 24 hours. This has been the case for about the last 4.5 billion years. As it does so, the Sun's energy falls on the portion of the Earth pointing towards it, heating that part of the Earth's surface providing warmth, light and energy, which in turn allows plants to photosynthesis and all organic life to proliferate and flourish." "In addition," he added, "the heating and cooling of the air above that particular part of the surface, coupled with the Earth's rotation, accounts in part for the various weather patterns around the globe that we are familiar with. All of these processes are constants, and have stabilised over the last few billion years, allowing life to evolve on Earth as we know it today."

"In short, the Earth has reached a balancing point or '*equilibrium*' if I may call it that, as it carries on with its slow and steady evolutionary journey."

"So, in relative terms, a patch of ground, one metre square on the Earth's surface, is exposed to sunlight for a pre-determined amount of time, that time being dependant on the season and where on Earth it is located, which in turn will determine the moment from when the Earth's rotation brings that patch of ground into contact with the Sun's radiation, until that same rotation takes the said patch of ground, outwith the Sun's radiation. Day and night if you like."

"Now, we know that complex computer modelling has proven that speeding up the Earth's rotation will have the effect of exposing that same patch of ground to relatively less solar energy due to its reduced time in the sunlight, resulting in cooling of the ground and subsequently a lower relative temperature in the air directly above it. Multiply this effect for every square metre of land on the Earth, and we upset the delicate '*equilibrium*', it has taken billions of years to achieve. This will result in rapid cooling of the planet and a significant decrease in the average global temperature, which in turn will affect the ocean currents that moderate the climate in certain parts of the world. And what's more is that this phenomenon effects dry land more than it effects similar parts of the Earth's surface covered by water and in actuality, depending on the magnitude of the change, has the propensity to plunge the entire globe into an irreversible crisis."

"That crisis being, and I say it again, a new Ice Age."

"And if that isn't enough," Wilson added, "as the Earth's surface becomes increasingly covered by snow and ice, more solar radiation is reflected back into space, exacerbating the problem and hastening the cooling effect. This has been studied before and is known to climate geologists and Astronomers as the 'Albedo effect'."

"Now, as I'm sure you all know, the Northern Hemisphere has more land mass than the Southern Hemisphere, so any such change will be felt more severely in the northern half of the globe than in the south, namely all of North America and Canada, all of Eastern and Western Europe, Scandinavia, Asia and all of the Russian sub-continent."

"That would leave Central America, Central Africa, Indonesia and Northern Australia still experiencing drastic change, but probably being the only remaining habitable areas of the planet."

Wilson at this juncture, and in an attempt to aid the understanding of the delegates, ran a simulation of a computer model on the screen which aptly illustrated his point. When the short simulation had ended, Wilson continued with the evidence in support of his conclusions.

"Now, you will recall the intelligence we were furnished with yesterday about the Tumeli house fire in central Africa a few months ago, that was mistaken for a rocket launch by our autonomous defence systems. Well, as it turns out, our systems were right to react in the way that they did! Scrutiny of satellite images of the former Tumeli residence, has revealed extreme burn patterns in the earth in the exact shape of the foundations of the structure that was formerly Tumeli's new mansion. And chemical analysis of samples taken from the area yesterday, months after the event, reveal traces of Ammonium Perchlorate and Atomised Aluminium."

Facing inquisitive looks from almost all of the delegation, Wilson quickly added, "Both of these chemicals are used in the construction of rocket propulsion systems in the USA, in fact as I am sure General Stiles will be able to confirm these chemicals, in the correct proportion, were the primary components of the fuel within the Solid Rocket Boosters (SRB's) used to propel NASA's space shuttles, clear of the Earths gravitational pull, and on into space."

General Washington Stiles, The Joint Chief of Space Operations who had already sat up at the mention of Ammonium Perchlorate, nodded his concurrence of this statement.

"Now it transpires that, in the case of the *Red Horse* pyramid, we now know that these chemicals were manufactured by Bectel at their factory in the Netherlands, and would have resembled a brown sludge that could easily be mistaken for liquid concrete. This mixture was then transported to West Africa as such, in a semi liquid state by Bectels own seagoing tanker fleet. Once at the West African port of Matadi, the mix was transferred to rail freight tankers, still purporting to be a special liquid concrete mix, before being shipped out to the site at Kisangani."

"This is where Tumeli comes in," Grant remarked, drawing the threads of this piece of the puzzle together.

"On Tumeli's instructions, his men hijacked one of these tankers, believing the contents to be high density liquid concrete, which

Tumeli subsequently used in the construction of the foundations of his new residence. And having done so it would appear that Tumeli, has unwitting built his family home on a foundation of Solid Rocket Booster propellant which, for all intents and purposes, looked and behaved like concrete. This explains why when it was accidentally ignited, our satellite defence system though it was detecting a rocket launch, and initiated our defence protocols."

"And this, ladies and gentlemen, accounts for why the Tumeli fire burned so brightly for so long, only extinguishing itself when all the propellant was spent."

Grant Wilson looked around the room and at the TV monitors, and if he had been asked to describe what he observed at that moment he would have said 'stunned disbelief'.

"So," Grant said, eager to keep everyone with him, "the *Red Horse* pyramid at Kisangani in the DRC is almost certainly filled with a mix of Ammonium Perchlorate and Atomized Aluminium, almost 242,000 cubic metres by my calculation, which in effect makes it a gigantic rocket motor which, once fully ignited, will burn and be unstoppable until all of its fuel is spent."

Once more, silence encompassed the whole meeting broken only by a question from General Stiles, the Chief of Space operations.

"And you are assuming that the three other pyramids contain the same type and amount of propellant as *Red Horse*?"

"Yes sir, I am," confirmed Wilson.

Professor Martin Plummer, the civilian Director of NASA, who had been scribbling calculations on a pad on the table in front of him proffered, "Then if that is so, according to my approximate calculations that would mean that each one of these pyramids has the same thrust potential as over 200 space shuttle launches, all occurring at the same time."

"246 shuttle launches, to be precise Mr Plummer," Wilson retorted, but delivering the correction in a respectful manner, "which, when ignited in unison, has enough energy to move an object with a mass of approximately 6.6 billion, trillion tons."

"The mass of the Earth!" Plummer replied, as the penny finally dropped, visibly horrified of the clarity now coming to the scenario with which he and his colleagues had been presented.

To aid the understanding of the less scientifically orientated government and defence officials Grant Wilson put the scenario into perspective. "If I may make a simplistic comparison?" he requested. "It is a bit like sticking a single firework rocket, the kind you would use to celebrate New Year, onto the back of a bus. You release the brakes on the bus, you ignite the firework and wait to see the bus move forward, however in this scenario nothing will appear to happen. The firework will burn and extinguish without any perceptible forward movement of the bus. "However," he went on. "If you were to calculate the mass of the bus and then provide enough fireworks to overcome the effects of the forces preventing the bus from moving, in this case gravity, and ignite them all at the same time, which is the key to the experiment, then the bus will begin to move forward until the chemical energy contained in the fireworks is exhausted. The amount, speed and duration of this movement will of course depend entirely on the carefully calculated amount of energy contained in the fireworks." "But crucially," he added, "all of the firework rockets must ignite and burn simultaneously in order to obtain the desired degree of movement of the bus."

"As I'm sure Professor Plummer will confirm," he said, motioning to the on screen image of the NASA Director, "my calculations indicate that when ignited, each of these pyramids will be capable of almost instantaneously producing its maximum thrust, which would be the equivalent of the energy of 120 atomic bombs, similar to that dropped on Hiroshima, detonating simultaneously but without the radioactive fallout, and then continuing to release their energy for a period of approximately 27 Minutes, and remember once fully ignited, they cannot be stopped."

"Now I know 27 minutes does not sound very long but precisely vectored, at the angle which will be determined by the remaining two sides of each pyramid structure, the thrust produced in 27 minutes should be enough to propagate a small increase in the rotational momentum of the Earth, and we need to remember here that the Earth is already spinning in space, measured at the equator to be about 1,670 kph."

"So, in essence what we are looking at with these numbers," Grant summarized, "is that these pyramids, if permitted to fulfil their function, will give the Earth a very small, but a very significant push in the same direction in which it is already rotating, which would see the Earths rotational speed increase by 40 kph to approximately 1,710 kph an increase of a mere 2.39%."

"Now, I know this does not sound a lot, but this minute change, which would be imperceptible to us anywhere on the Earth's surface, is enough to upset the delicate equilibrium our planet has achieved, crucially shortening our standard Earth Day by approximately 38 minutes, creating a new Earth Day of 23 hours and 22 minutes."

"This eventuality, which would effectively mean the end of the four seasons as we know them, would also see within one year, the permanent northern polar ice cap, extend southwards to somewhere around Madrid, and the southern ice extend north to somewhere around Madagascar, bringing eternal winter to most of the Northern and Southern Hemispheres."   Adding, "which in consequence, would result in the death of over five billion people, effectively reducing the world's population to three billion, a figure last reached in 1960, and in the process herald in a new Ice Age, last experienced between 100,000 and 25,000 years ago."

"This, ladies and gentlemen, in order to reverse the effects of global warming, is what Harrison Becker is planning to achieve."

Chapter 22

The CIA Director, Alfonso DeSouza, who had marginally more time to come to terms with the revelation than most, breaking the silence spoke out.

"Commodore Wilson. Like my colleagues, I am dumbfounded to learn that such a scheme is even possible, let alone that it is now being identified as an imminent threat to our way of life. You have imparted to us the how, the where and the why. May I assume that you are going to tell us the when?"

"Yes sir," Wilson replied. "I was just coming to that."

"It is my belief that, to achieve its goal, Bectel has designated a time and a date for the synchronised ignition of the technology within these structures."

"As we have already established, the West Kalimantan government in Indonesia have been given a handover date when they believe their power station, the *Pale Horse* pyramid, will have completed its safety trials and go live, and that date is the 20th March 2022. This date has been agreed to by the Indonesians, as it appears to be a credible time frame for the commissioning and stress testing of the alleged nuclear power facility within, and would rationalise the lack of access to the structure by anyone other than Bectel staff."

"As it happens however, the 20th March 2022 has another special significance."

"As I alluded to earlier, our Earth takes approximately one year to complete its journey around the sun. Additionally, and I am sure we are all aware that the orbital path taken by the Earth on this journey is elliptical in nature which, when considered alongside the Earths 23.5-degree tilt, accounts in part for the four seasons we experience."

"Now for the Northern Hemisphere the Earth is closer to the sun in summer, slightly further away in winter and approximately equidistant at the points which mark the beginning of Spring and Autumn respectively, known to Astronomers as the 'Equinoxes'."

"To be most effective at bringing on a new Ice Age, simultaneous ignition of the pyramids is unlikely to happen in our summertime," referring to the summertime in the Northern Hemisphere, "as the Earth will have been heated, receiving the Sun's energy for several months, that accumulation of heat having to be overcome before global cooling could take place. Likewise in the Autumn, where the same effect will be even more apparent."

"It is my determination that, following the natural cooling of the Earth in the seasonal Northern Hemispherical winter period, the most effective time to initiate a global cooling event will be just before the Sun's energy begins to warm the planet surface again, as part of the natural cycle of the seasons."

"The Spring Equinox!" General Stiles concluded.

"Exactly," confirmed Wilson, "which this year will occur at 0937hrs GMT on Sunday 20th March 2022, which, as you now know, is precisely the date given to the Indonesians for the handover of their facility, and a mere 43 days from now."

At the conclusion of these revelations by Wilson the assembly again descended into uproar for the next thirty or so minutes. Localised debates broke out, arguments took place and specialists from both sides of the Atlantic questioned Wilson's calculations and conclusions, demanding answers, all of which were competently addressed.

The time in the COBRA briefing room was just approaching 11.00pm and tempers were fraying when Connie Chapelton again called the meeting to order.

"Ladies and gentlemen," she said, looking somewhat bedraggled.

"You have heard all the arguments, counter arguments, theory's, hypothesis and projections and it would be both unwise and unproductive to deny it any longer. The threat posed by Bectel is plausible, it is real and it is happening, and we have 43 days to come up with an effective strategy to do something about it. I intend to close this meeting now in order that we can get some rest but more importantly, so that we can consult with our respective experts and strategists and come up with a viable solution to this dilemma."

"Alfonso," she said, too tired to observe formalities, and directing her gaze at the CIA chief and the entire American delegation. "Shall we meet the day after tomorrow, at 7.00pm UK time, to discuss how we are to respond to this?" "Also," she added, "I would deem it prudent for you to conscript to the table, any of your people who have the capacity to devise a way out of this, and of course for me to do likewise. I don't care if it is an established policy, a published thesis or something that someone, somewhere has scribbled on the back of a cocktail napkin. We need to consider everything. Please just ensure that your conscripts are equipped with the necessary security clearance."

All parties being in agreement the PM closed the meeting.

As the screen went blank and the delegates filed out of the COBRA office, the Prime Minister made a phone call to her personal secretary to arrange a meeting for 7.00pm the following evening, where she intended to part brief the heads of the UK's devolved governments.

Muting, the telephone receiver with her hand she said to Wilson, the only other occupant of the room, "I'm also going to have to speak with the Chinese and Russians on this." Putting the telephone receiver back in range of her voice she made a further request of her secretary. "Also contact the Chinese and Russian Ambassadors, and set me two separate meetings for the day after tomorrow, early afternoon, 12.30pm and 2.30pm ought to do it, Chinese first."

She hung up the telephone and with her colleague, left the room for some much needed, rest and recouperation. Wilson did likewise, instructing his driver to convey him to the Chesterfield.

Chapter 23

7.00pm, 7 February 2022, London

Two days after the delivery of Wilson's shattering conclusions to the group, the crisis conference had reconvened at 7.00pm, with the hope and purpose of finding the solution to the Bectel created, global catastrophe in waiting.

Present in London and in Virginia were the same delegates as before however on both sides of the Atlantic additional scientists, engineers and strategists were also in attendance, mainly in supporting roles and to provide immediate access to expert information in the discipline that each practiced. These men and women were the best in their field at what each of them did and, of all times in the history of the world, now was the time to prove it.

Prior to the commencement of the meeting, all delegates were supplied with nine different scenario's that were favoured as the likely best fit solutions to the forthcoming apocalypse, however due to time constraints and by agreement on both sides, five of these scenarios were discounted prior to the commencement of the meeting, the remaining four options being the subject of the business at hand.

As the screen came to life at the appointed hour the UK Prime Minister, Connie Chapelton, provided a comprehensive recap on the current situation. Having done so she turned the floor over to her MI6 chief to lead the remainder of the discussion.

"So," Marcella Houston began. "Events are moving quickly and we find ourselves in a dynamic situation requiring immediate and decisive action."

Marcella went on to outline each of the four feasible remaining responses, and headed the debate which discussed the positive and negative aspects each had to offer. The discussions took place in a deliberate and professional manner, until one option emerged as the choice with the highest probability of success and the lowest estimation of collateral damage.

"If I may summarise then," Marcella Houston continued, "so that we have this right in our heads, as the world will hold us to account for the course of action we are about to endorse."

"Of the remaining four options we are rejecting option one, which is attempting to reason with Harrison Becker." "That ship has sailed," she said, relying on an age-old nautical metaphor to illustrate her point, "as revealing our position to him could result in a pre-emptive ignition of the pyramid structures."

"Likewise, option two is not feasible as we do not have the time to secure a unilateral *emissions reduction compliance agreement* from all of the world's major economies, that would be sufficient to satisfy Becker enough to 'call it off'."

"We are also discounting option three, a full tactical nuclear strike on each structure in an attempt to destroy each of them outright, as the collateral damage and loss of life from such action would be too great a loss to bear."

"Which leaves us with option four."

"Neutralise the nature of the propellant contained in the pyramids so that they cannot ignite, thereby preventing the crisis."

"This," Marcella reminded the company, "is the action we all agree has the greatest probability of success with the lowest risk of significant and lasting collateral damage."

Grant Wilson interposed in support of his colleague. "However, it must be emphasised that the neutralization process will have to occur simultaneously at each of the four sites, as any one or more of these structures igniting as planned would have a similar, albeit significantly lesser effect on the Earth's rotation."

"And, as COSI Houston has just alluded to." Wilson advised, "Even though we have a pre-planned optimum ignition date for these structures to operate to their best effect, Becker will no doubt be able to override the process at the press of a button, should he suspect we are on to him."

"And, as we are close enough to the spring equinox as would make little difference to the outcome, I cannot emphasise enough, the need for absolute secrecy and immediate definitive action."

After a short period of debate on each side of the screen, the CIA chief spoke out.

"I ask the question on behalf of my colleagues stateside on how option four, *'neutralization'*, is to be achieved?"

"Perhaps I can steer you towards the answer to that, sir," Wilson replied, choosing his words carefully.

"First of all, may I introduce you to Miss Ekaja Chopra. She is a professor at Oxford university and one of the experts we have drafted in to assist us. She is currently head of nuclear medicine at Oxford, she has a doctorate in nuclear chemistry and is currently working on a thesis that will counter the negative effects of radiation on the human body in relation to extended space travel. I have discussed our current situation with her in some detail and would ask that she be permitted to speak, as you are going to want to hear what she has to say."

Ekaja Chopra was the only child of Manish and Dayamai Chopra, who relocated to the UK 22 years previously, from their home in southwest India. Ekaja was born with a cleft pallet, a condition which, if left untreated, would have meant a lifetime of exclusion and poverty in her home country. When she was just six months old her parents, through a worldwide charity funding programme, were offered the opportunity of lifechanging surgery for their daughter's condition. Her parents accepted the offer and took their infant daughter to the UK for the operation, which was extremely successful. Following her surgery, Ekaja's parents applied for, and were granted, residency in the UK and made their home in the small town of Aylesbury, located just north west of London. There the family settled and her father, a skilled Baker, had set up his own successful artisan bread business which allowed the family to prosper, accumulating sufficient wealth to allow them the prospect of sending their gifted daughter to university.

Top academical grades throughout her school life had brought her to the attention of many sponsors interested in her academic career and, not surprisingly, her subsequent request to be accepted at Oxford university was eagerly accepted. Ekaja's academic qualifications from Oxford were a great source of pride to her parents, and were completely contrary to the life which would have awaited her had her birth condition gone untreated in India.

Her academic career on the ascent, Ekaja was now 23 years old, 5 foot 5 inches tall, she had jet black, collar length, shiny straight hair and habitually wore large round black rimmed spectacles. She first met Grant Wilson at a seminar for gifted children in London some ten years earlier and, as Wilson had taken a liking to her soft and pleasant demeanour, they had stayed in touch. It was Wilson who offered her parents his mentorship for the duration of her education, however long that may be, and the Chopra family had been friends with him ever since.

Dressed in a baggy beige woollen jumper, way too large for her slender frame, and dark cotton leggings, Ekaja stepped up to the conference table at Wilson's introduction. Although naturally pretty she maintained a 'geek like' demeanour that was intended to ward off any romantic interest from members of the opposite sex.

Although her reconstructive facial surgery had been a complete success, Ekaja was still mindful of a very small scar that crossed from her top lip to the base of her nose, and tended to shy this aspect of her face away from people and cameras. Even though her dark skin tone rendered this scar virtually invisible, she was still nonetheless extremely self-conscious of its effect on her appearance.

The Prime minister motioned to Ekaja to face the screens and encouraged her to speak clearly and begin.

"Miss Chopra, the world is listening. If you will, please?" said the PM.

"Good afternoon, ladies and gentlemen," she began tentatively. Despite her intellectual talent Ekaja was not used to the spotlight and was justifiably nervous, as in academic terms she was now speaking to some of the world's greatest thinkers.

Shooting a glance at Commodore Wilson, looking for reassurance she began. "I have been made aware of the circumstances that have given rise to this meeting, and although I am not privy to the entire facts of the situation, I have been asked by Grant...." she corrected herself quickly, blushing that her familiarity with her sponsor would betray the massive crush she had on him.

"I am so sorry. I meant to say I have been asked by Commodore Wilson, to render my opinion on the *'trans modification of the atomic structure of particles and their properties, by nuclear radiation,'* which by happy coincidence is the subject of a dissertation I completed in my early years at Oxford," by which she meant three years ago, when she was just twenty.

As Ekaja spoke, an aid operated a presentation on the screen which showed formulae and chemical diagrams of various elements and compounds which were relevant to the subject under discussion, particularly those used in the formation of Ammonium Perchlorate, and included comprehensive details on its effects when mixed with Atomized Aluminium. She spoke with skill and at a level which all attendees could comprehend, on the effects that certain types of radiation would have on these substances, answering questions from experts on both sides of the screen effortlessly and with a very high degree of competence.

"So," she said pulling the threads of her summary together. "The answer to the big question you face is, yes." "It is possible to denature the exothermic properties of Ammonium Perchlorate and Atomized Aluminium by the close proximity detonation of a low yield, Cobalt-Radium, nuclear device."

"To effect this change on the quantity of material you are talking about and render it inert, I would suggest that each site would require a device containing somewhere between 8 – 10kg of Cobalt-Radium."

"Thank you, Ekaja." the Prime Minister cut in, motioning for Ekaja to sit, concluding her role in the crisis.

"Alberto. Your observations on this aspect of the discussion please?" she said directing her request at the CIA Chief.

DeSouza replied promptly. "Nuclear Chemistry is a bit outwith my experience I'm afraid however if I may defer to my colleague?" motioning to his nuclear fission expert, Dr Phillipa Farnham, to take the floor.

Dr Farnham, who had been scribbling calculations on a pad, in front of her as Ekaja spoke, now stood up to face the camera stateside and spoke. "I have been checking the formula and the calculations based on Professor Chopra's presentation and I concur. A device containing 9.26kg of nuclear material of the type specified, will be sufficient to neutralise the estimated amount of Ammonium Perchlorate contained at each site, and," she added, "in addition to a narrow dispersal characteristic, the radioactive half-life of the nuclear material is short, so will dissipate quickly, nominally within a matter of two to three months."

"Thank you for confirming that Dr Farnham," Connie Chapelton replied continuing on. "So, ladies and gentlemen. It appears that we have been presented with a viable solution. We must now devise the manner in which we are to deliver that solution, simultaneously to four different targets, 10,000km apart, in different time zones and in absolute secrecy."

"Before we do so," she added, "I must inform you all that I have spoken with both the Chinese and Russian Ambassadors, this very afternoon, and made them aware of the current threat, and the implications for the planet should Becker succeed in his mission. I took this action with the knowledge and consent of my colleague Mr DeSouza because, as pointed out by Commodore Wilson in his analysis, both of these nations are those likely to be affected most by rapid global cooling. Please let the record show that both of these nations' leaders are now aware, as I have personally short briefed their Ambassadors."

She went on further to say, "I have not however informed either nation of how we intend to tackle this crisis. Firstly, as at the time of our meeting I did not know how we were going to do that, and secondly, to do so would risk the information being leaked and Becker carrying out a pre-emptive strike." DeSouza nodded from the other side of the screen, confirming his knowledge and complicity in this course of action.

"That said," the PM added further, "both China and Russia have advised that they are willing to assist in any way that they can."

"If, and it is a big if, we collectively decide that we need their assistance then it will be an 'eleventh hour' decision, only making them fully aware of what we are up against at the last possible moment."

"So, ladies and gentlemen. There you have it. Before the end of this day, we must agree on how we are to deliver these weapons to their intended targets in the manner I have just outlined, and for operational reasons, I deem it essential that the weapon strike must be carried out simultaneously and exclusively, by either British or American assets."

Chapter 24

For the next four hours punctuated only by a brief supper break, the delegates on both sides of the Atlantic, led by Constance Chapelton, fiercely debated a solution for the simultaneous delivery of the low yield nuclear material that would neutralise the solid fuel, currently primed for ignition and stored within each of Bectel's four pyramids.

It was now 11.30pm and Connie Chapelton, chairing what was probably the most important meeting in the history of modern government, glanced at the proposed solution to the world threat posed by Bectel, and drawing the threads of the discussion to a conclusion, she stood up in front of the camera, so that she was clearly visible to all, and began.

"So let me just confirm then," she said, addressing the whole meeting, and relieving her dry throat by sipping from a bottle of water.

"We have collectively decided that the nuclear device needed to neutralise the fuel component of each of the four pyramids will be delivered by a missile, predominantly launched from fighter aircraft, but in one case, a submarine?"

"Yes, Madam Prime Minister," Alberto DeSouza replied. "We have concluded that precise positioning of the launch capability platforms is the best way of synchronising impact times at each target location.

Nominated by the CIA chief to speak, General Chet Andersson, the US Chief of Air Force entered the debate with the precise details of the weapons systems.

Andersson went on to describe that in three of the four strikes, the delivery platform would be fighter aircraft which would fire The AGM 158B JASSM-ER air launch cruise missile, a tried and tested weapons system that came into service with the USAF in 2014 and is an update of the standard JASSM cruise missile introduced in 2003, but with an extended range capability of 920km. The missile, with its 4.3m length and 2.4m fold out wingspan, can readily be launched from an aircraft and is equipped with a blast fragmentation warhead, ideal for penetrating the half metre thick concrete western face of each pyramid. The missile itself is capable of a payload of up to 450kg, well in excess of the 9.26kg warhead that would soon be fitted.

"For the remaining strike," the General revealed, "we will utilise submarine launched 'Cruise Missiles', to be fired from the USS Virginia, which is currently on patrol in the Western Pacific.

Drilling down his brief to specifics of the strike, General Andersson continued; "Firstly, the mission to neutralise the propellant in the pyramids and prevent the global catastrophe we have been discussing, will hereinafter be referred to as;

Operation *'Colourfield'*

"Next, and to ensure absolute success of this mission, we have established a redundancy protocol. It is our intention to launch two identical aircraft or missiles, similarly armed and from each location, directing both towards each target, timed to strike at 60 second intervals. In the event of any failure in the primary strike weapon, the secondary weapon will deliver the same payload."

"The coordination and control team will be based at Langley, and will know if the plan has been effective immediately the first missiles impact on their target, as the radioactive footprint from the detonation will be detectable from military satellites, monitoring the entire operation in real time. We fully anticipate that the primary warheads will be effective and that being the case, the secondary weapons will immediately be aborted."

Supplementing the information that he had already given, the General added some additional details;

"In the case of *Red Horse*, we intend to use two American B2 Bombers, fitted with AGM 158B JASSM-ER missiles that will neutralise the fuel within the structure at Kisangani in Africa. They will launch from the US airbase, Camp Lemonnier in Djibouti, in the horn of Africa. Their stealth capability will be invaluable as they will require to overfly several countries airspace, in order to affect a tactical approach on their target undetected."

"For *Black Horse*, the Aircraft Carrier USS Ronald Reagan will position in the Pacific, approximately 500 miles west of Ecuador, from where two American F18 'Super Hornets' will launch and deliver the same weapons to the structure at Quito."

"Similarly," he continued, "the British Carrier, HMS Queen Elizabeth, will take position in the Java Sea, 100 miles to the north east of Jakarta, from where two British F35 Lightening fighter aircraft will deliver their payload of identical missiles to the *Pale Horse* pyramid at Pontianak."

"And finally," he added "in relation to the *White Horse* pyramid at Kiritimati, the nuclear submarine USS Virginia will deploy her warheads on specially adapted cruise missiles, from a location in the south Pacific, approximately 200 miles west of their target."

"We have also concluded," the General went on, "that in the event the pyramids are ignited manually by Becker, a missile strike with the Cobalt-Radium device within the first few moments of operation will neutralise any unspent fuel stored in the pyramid, rendering it immediately inert and effectively 'putting out the fire', so to speak, which will afford us a small margin of error."

"Modification of the eight standard nuclear warheads with their new Cobalt-Radium payload is currently taking place at Norfolk Naval Station in Virginia, and will be fully completed in no later than four hours from the present time, with the missiles being available for transportation shortly thereafter."

"From a transport logistical viewpoint," he added before the question arose, "The British aircraft carrier, HMS Queen Elizabeth is currently off the west coast of Australia, and will be in position in the Java Sea in about 28 hours."

"The carrier, USS Ronald Reagan is currently on exercise in the South Pacific and is expected to be on station in no more than 48 hours from this time."

"Both carriers will have the specially modified warheads delivered by helicopter from a strategic location close to, and somewhere along their current global trajectory. The B2's will receive their armaments within 24 hours as they will be delivered directly by transport aircraft to Camp Lemonnier."

"The submarine USS Virginia, currently on patrol just south of Japan, will surface at a pre-arranged secret rendezvous point to receive her armaments by helicopter before submerging and proceeding to her launch location."

"The whole operation will be conducted in the utmost secrecy, with the flight crews not being aware of their intended target until they are in the air. Likewise, the submarine crew will only receive their target package information thirty minutes before launch, which will be ample time to 'spool up' their missiles."

"Once the first flight takes to the air, the entire operation will be coordinated from CIA HQ in Langley." Approaching the end of his briefing the General continued; "The target time for the missile strike is set to occur in just under five days' time, agreed to be 0530hrs GMT on 12 February. The aircraft and submarine will have their take off or launch times carefully synchronised, in order that each platform's individual 'time to target' computes accordingly."

As General Andersson concluded his brief, Connie Chapelton once again took to the floor.

"Thank you General," she began. "Once we have successfully neutralised the threat," she said confidently, "a worldwide manhunt will be initiated to locate and apprehend Harrison Becker and his executive group, where they will face an international court trial for conspiracy to commit mass murder, and other crimes against humanity."

"This by far a 'done deal' ladies and gentleman," she went on to say, grabbing and refocusing the attention of the entire group of delegates on both sides of the Atlantic. "If we fail." she said solemnly, "billions of our fellow human beings will perish in the winter that results from this event, and society will break down, turning countryman against countryman as their survival instincts begin to take over."

"If, however we succeed, and I am pleased to report that this mission carries a very high probability of success, it is very likely that the world will never know what we have accomplished here. Not for a long, long time anyway," she added ruefully. Continuing, she went on, "I have of course discussed this extraordinary situation with Mr DeSouza and we both agree that full lockdown protocols will be initiated the evening before the strike and remain in force until this crisis is over.

With that Connie Chapelton concluded the meeting for a recess, at which point the delegates on both sides of the Atlantic filed out to nearby offices and chambers, to embark upon their appointed tasks.

"Prime Minister!" Grant Wilson called, still sitting at his place at the cabinet table and apparently doodling on a paper pad. "Could I have a word in private please?" and added, "Chief Houston, you might want to be in on this too."

When the three were alone he began. "I'm going to have to run something past you, as I have identified an alternative scenario which although unlikely, still cannot be ruled out." The three sat silently around Grant Wilson's place at the table whilst the Commodore outlined his latest revelation, that was again so drastic that both women had difficulty in accepting what the top strategist had just outlined as an alternative likely scenario.

"You are positive about this Grant?" the Prime Minister asked exasperated, her voice betraying the exhaustion her mind was experiencing.

"You know me, Connie," replied the Commodore. "Nothing is positive, but as these events reach a climax this scenario, unlikely as it is, cannot be ruled out."

By the following day the meetings were shorter in duration but increased in frequency, taking place every 12 hours. At the 8.00pm session that evening, General Andersson reported to the conference that the Cobalt-Radium warheads, which had been modified as instructed, were now in transit and on their way in to their respective destinations, where they would soon be fitted to their individual delivery platforms.

Operation *Colourfield* was on schedule and would begin as soon as the first aircraft left the tarmac, and the strike which would define its conclusion, planned for 5.30am GMT, Saturday 12 February 2022, was now just over 81 hours away.

Connie Chapelton kept the 12 hourly meetings concise so that all delegates could receive adequate food and rest in order to remain focussed.

Chapter 25

9 February 2022

It was a cool Wednesday evening in Kinshasa, Capital city of the DRC and in the high-rise government building located in the centre district of the city, the normal working day was over. It was almost 6.30pm and all but a handful of offices were in darkness, their interiors indistinguishable against the advancing darkness.

One such office still in use was that of Hermus Safi, the government minister for National Development who was as usual putting in extra hours at the office, leading by example with the kind of work ethic that he expected from his senior executives. Safi's office was on the top floor of the building and had a vista that commanded exquisite views over the west of the city and the deep orange glow marking the last rays of the rapidly setting Sun. To capitalise on these views, the buildings Architects had thoughtfully ensured that the exterior of the structure was entirely clad in one inch thick, plate glass panelling, which for those inside provided a floor to ceiling panoramic view of the ever-expanding metropolis, that was the capital, and economic heartland of the DRC.

Safi sat at his desk, working diligently on one of the many government reports in his basket, an onyx table lamp with an iconic green glass shade bathing his workspace in a warm white light. On his desk sat a glass cup of steaming black tea, complete with a slice of lemon and containing a spoon, an old habit of Safi's, which he insisted aided the infusion to cool quicker to an acceptable drinking temperature. Behind him was a large print of the current New York skyline, with the Statue of Liberty featuring prominently in the foreground. Safi had visited New York several times in his lifetime, both before and after the terrorist attacks of 9/11, and although it was a world apart from his native Kinshasa, it was his favourite city.

Safi himself was an advocate of American democracy and was proud that the incumbent president of the DRC, his cousin Hinshi Womboto, embraced the same principles in his party's quest to bring wealth and prosperity to all of his people. This popularist view was not shared by all, and Womboto's government had their critics however on the whole, and with the significant political Kudos that followed in the wake of the commencement of the hospital complex project up at Kisangani, the Womboto regime was on the ascent with few serious political rivals.

At that very same moment, 1,000 metres away on the roof top of a building directly west of Safi's office, preparations were being made by a stranger in the gathering darkness, preparations which would soon bring the government minister's life to a swift and untimely conclusion.

Gogol, Bectel's secret assassin, did not know Safi, his family, or his politics nor did he care. He was a consummate professional and entirely focused on his present mission. Cold, calculating and completely devoid of emotion were just some of his traits, and just a few of the reasons why he never took a wife or desired to father any children, both of which could potentially be used to compromise him.

As the darkness advanced further upon the city, Gogol's target, sitting in his plush office sipping tea, became relatively brighter and more obvious.

Dressed in a dark blouson jacket and dark trousers and virtually invisible between the air conditioning units on the rooftop, Gogol was preparing a Barrett M95, matt black sniper rifle, his weapon of choice for long range sniping.

Launched in USA in 1995 and still in service with military forces around the world today, the M95 weighs in at 10.7kg and is a bolt action sniper rifle with a 29-inch barrel. Equipped with a five round magazine and boasting a muzzle velocity of 2,800 feet per second, the weapon has an effective killing range of over 2,000 metres. To compliment the weapon, Gogol favoured a high magnification Steiner T5XI scope, with a 5-25 x 56 magnification, which he was presently focusing on his target.

The rifle magazine contained five, 0.5 BMG calibre, 12.7mm black tipped armour piercing M2 bullets, only one of which would be required by the expert operator on this occasion. Normally employed to pierce light armoured vehicles and protective shelters, the 'black tips' would have no problem penetrating the plate glass walls of Safi's office and still have enough energy to maintain their trajectory, allowing them to strike their intended target with pinpoint accuracy and devastating effect.

With the weapon now pointing directly at Safi, held stable thanks to the bi pod legs projecting downwards at the base of the barrel, Gogol had been watching his quarry for a few minutes, allowing his heart rate to stabilise and his breathing to slow down in order to ensure an accurate shot. Safi, unaware that his image was being centred in the crosshairs of an assassin's rifle, was sitting at his desk in a white, long sleeved tailored shirt and colourful tie, his jacket hanging up neatly on a nearby coat stand in a corner of his office. Slightly hunched over a document, he was engrossed in its contents which, as his killer had established, he would sit up from periodically in order to take a sip of his tea.

Gogol, in his dark eyrie was now totally focused on his task and with his heart rate and respiration fully settled, he removed the safety catch from his weapon in readiness for firing, waiting in the darkness like a coiled Cobra ready to strike.

As anticipated, Safi momentarily sat upright in his chair and reached his left hand out towards his steaming beverage, drawing what would be his final breath, at which point Gogol squeezed the trigger. As the plate glass wall of his office shattered, Safi did not even have time to acknowledge the commotion as the M2 bullet ripped through his throat killing him instantly, the cup and spoon falling to the desk, spilling its contents over the polished wood before dripping to the floor.

Within moments of the shot, Gogol had the weapon packed and was making his way downwards into the darkness and towards his next intended target.

Although he would be long gone by the time the body of Safi was discovered, Gogol was certain that the trajectory of the fatal bullet would soon be ascertained by local law enforcement, which in turn would lead directly to the rooftop, therefore he was careful to purposefully catch the sleeve of his blouson on one of the nearby air conditioning units, in the knowledge that analysis of the fabric would reveal that it was a particular weave, favoured by the Chinese Secret Service.

As he made his way out of the city, Gogol's intended route passed a primary school in one of the less affluent suburbs of the city. Pausing only to throw a petrol bomb into the porch area of the wooden structure, he watched the building rapidly ignite in the rear-view mirror as he drove away in his dilapidated, non-descript delivery van.

A trifle low tech, he thought to himself, but sufficient enough to cast the shadow of blame to one of Tumeli's many rivals.

Chapter 26

As Gogol made his way towards a safe house in the Ngomba quarter, in the south east of the city, he pulled into an all-night gas station to refuel his van and pick up some food. The gas station had an adjacent snack bar which served grocery items and both hot and cold beverages. Having fuelled up, Gogol selected a kosher cheese baguette sandwich from the deli counter and a large bottle of sparkling mineral water to wash it down with. As the premises was not busy, he decided to 'sit in' to consume his snack, and chose one of the high tables set back from the window but which still provided a good view of the car parking area.

Gogol's choice of table afforded him direct line of sight to his van, where the M95 rifle used in the Safi assassination lay in a plain black bag in the rear load area of the vehicle. Whilst he ate, a garbage truck entered the fuel station and paused momentarily, blocking his view of his van, whilst the operatives emptied the bins on the garage forecourt. Seconds later the garbage truck and the operatives moved off, exiting the station and on to the remainder of their evenings work.

About fifteen minutes later and suitably refreshed, Gogol returned to his vehicle and as he entered the van his senses immediately jumped to high alert, as he noticed a small, non-descript white envelope on the passenger seat of his van. The envelope was about the size of a standard letter and it was sealed and completely blank except for the number 350112 written in black ink across its front face.

Gogol immediately glanced into the rear of his vehicle and confirmed the M95 was still where he had left it, apparently unmolested. Acutely aware that he had been comprised and that he was probably being watched, he made no sudden moves. Cautiously he picked up the envelope and glanced at the number, the significance of which was known to only to a select few people. The owner of this envelope clearly knew who and what he was, and Gogol was in absolutely no doubt that this message was meant for him, as clear as if it had been addressed to Mr Uri Hazan, Former Mossad agent turned corporate assassin. But what was it doing here? A range of possibilities flashed through Gogol's mind, the uppermost of which was an attempt on his own life, however he quickly reasoned this as unlikely as he rationalised that if he were the author of such a message and his intent was elimination, the recipient of the envelope would be dead by now.

Deciding to play the situation out, Gogol picked up the envelope and holding it up against the garage forecourt lights, he could clearly see that it contained nothing more than a small rectangular card. Keeping the envelope above the level of the dashboard, in order that whoever may be watching him could see his actions, he opened it to find that the paper card contained the handwritten internet address of what appeared to be an online chatroom. Gogol stuffed both the card and the envelope into his shirt breast pocket for later examination, and left the gas station driving normally and in a manner that would not draw attention to himself.

As he drove, Gogol considered the actuality that his normal communications channels had been compromised and the possibility that his superiors were trying to contact him with some vital information in an unconventional manner that would be more difficult for law enforcement authorities to trace.

Taking such factors into consideration, he made the decision to drive his van north of the city near to the airport, where he turned east down a small service road to the 'Ile des Pecheurs', an area adjacent to the River Congo, where he promptly dumped the M95 and his satellite phone into the river and beyond reach. He then drove into Kinshasa city centre where he abandoned his van in a side street with the key still in the ignition, in the full knowledge that some of the city's 'night time' inhabitants would discover the vehicle and think that Christmas had come early. "That should take care of any potential tracking devices," he thought to himself. Following default protocols, Gogol recalled that there was an alternative safe house at Kimbwala, in the west side of the city, which was now his intended destination and where he could report in and relay recent events.

He decided he would lose any potential 'tail' by mingling with the inhabitants of Kinshasa's night scene and at once headed off for the city centre with its many clubs, bars and cafes. Once in the heart of the city, which was teaming with revellers and patrons of the various entertainment establishments, Gogol employed his considerable knowledge of anti-surveillance techniques. After a short journey of 'dummy runs' and 'double backs' and confident that he was not being followed, Gogol entered an internet café, where he ordered a large coffee and booked some time at an anonymous computer terminal, located towards the rear of the establishment.

The machine he chose was facing the entrance and afforded him an immediate and unobstructed view of anyone who entered the premises, but was far enough away from the windows and off the route to the restrooms where patrons of the café could not inadvertently glance over his shoulder. As an extra level of security, he kept his fully loaded Sig Sauer M17, 9mm pistol in the waistband of his trousers, concealed by his baggy cotton shirt.

Working with complete anonymity, Gogol logged on to the chatroom indicated on the card that had been contained in the envelope, and was immediately directed to a webpage called

'*Funtime*'. Outwardly the homepage of *Funtime* looked like any other run of the mill chatroom page however the information menu indicted that there was only one other user online, certainly an unusual situation for this type of platform. Certain that he appeared to be in the right place, in just a few short mouse clicks Gogol was urged to 'sign up or log on', and having selected 'log on', he was prompted to enter a username and password. He thought for a moment then entered his old Israeli forces identification number of 350112 into both boxes, immediately opening the page on a private chatroom, where the only other occupant, who identified themselves as '*blinkrate*', immediately began to type a message.

Gogol then began a 'chat' with *blinkrate*, assimilating the contents of the messages which passed between the two and sat aghast, extremely concerned at what he was reading. After just thirty minutes on this forum, all relevant information having being passed on, *blinkrate* then signed off. Gogol having acquired all the necessary intelligence on his new target did likewise, logging off of the computer.

As he prepared to leave the café, Gogol took a small aerosol from his pocket and sprayed the keyboard of the machine he had been using, with a fine mist that would erase his fingerprints from the device. His mind awash with possibilities he stood up, looking around carefully to ensure that none of the other patrons in the room were paying undue attention to him and, dropping his partially full, but now cold, paper coffee cup into the dustbin he left, disappearing into the night.

Travelling on a local night bus, he arrived at the alternate safe house in Kimbwala about fifty minutes later where he acquired an encrypted satellite phone, money, documentation, weapons and other resources that he would require to book and board a flight to Europe, the following day. Unlocking the satellite phone, Gogol placed a call to his superior Stanley Harding during which he received vital information which confirmed to him the location of his next target.

Flying out of N'djili International Airport at lunchtime the following day, February 10, and under the assumed name of Bernard Deauchamp, Gogol's initial destination was Paris, where he would catch a connecting flight to Lyon in western France, a stepping point to the location of his next mission.

Arriving at Lyon-Saint Exupery Airport at 10pm, security executive Bernard Deauchamp, dressed in a dark business suit and carrying a black leather attaché case, disembarked his Air France flight and headed to the concourse, where he rented a luxury saloon car that would enable him to reach his final destination, where his next target was scheduled to host a meeting the following evening. Leaving the airport, Deauchamp drove north east for about thirty minutes where he booked himself an overnight stop at a small traditional hotel in the small town of Chateaux-Gaillard in western France, just off the main A42 Autoroute towards Switzerland. Here he would spend the night prior to completing the remainder of his journey the following day, arriving at the luxurious Ritz Carlton Hotel de la Paix in central Geneva around mid-day.

Meanwhile back in London at the 8pm meeting on the 10th of February, Marcella Houston updated the group on raw intelligence that had just come into her possession regarding the assassination of Hermus Safi, at his office in Kinshasa. She reminded the group that Safi was the government minister who Benjamin Ngoy worked for, prior to his assassination in September 2020.

"Initial reports indicate," she said, "that the government minister was killed whilst working late in his office, by an as yet unknown assailant, using a high-powered rifle, fired from a rooftop nearby. We understand that, having established the location of the gunman, evidence was collected from the scene which suggests that the assassin was connected to the Chinese Secret Service and at present, carefully orchestrated 'diplomatic' enquiries have been initiated into the incident."

Connie Chapelton thanked the MI6 chief for the update and, keeping her focus current, arranged their final session for 8.00pm GMT, Friday 11 February, where the delegates on both sides of the Atlantic would remain on post until operation *Colourfield* was completed and the pyramids neutralised.

It was late afternoon in Geneva on 11th February 2022 and, having checked into his hotel room, Gogol began to prepare the materials and equipment that he would require to complete his mission.

As early evening descended on the city, Gogol changed into smart casual clothing and carrying nothing but a small brown leather flight bag, took up a position in the opulent surroundings of the Ritz Carlton's lobby, taking observations on all who entered and left the establishment.

Two hours and several coffees later, Gogol observed the man who he believed to be his primary target enter the hotel, accompanied by a hotel porter carrying his luggage. Having checked in at the desk, the man made his way to the penthouse suite, where a party of guests awaited his arrival.

Chapter 27

It was now the evening of 11th February 2022 and almost 8.00pm in the UK. The British and American Intelligence services were about to convene and begin their final meeting in London and Langley, which would see them through to the conclusion of operation *Colourfield.*

In the hotel Ritz Carlton de la Paix in Geneva, it was 9.00pm Central European time, and now in disguise and wearing a dark wig and moustache, Gogol entered the hotel elevator and headed for the penthouse suite. Removing a white hotel staff tunic from his bag, a garment that he had acquired by stealth earlier that evening, he changed in the elevator. Taking his plastic polymer Sig Sauer automatic pistol from the bag, a weapon that he had brought undetected through airport security, he placed it in the rear waistband of his trousers covered over by the tunic, and left the elevator one floor below his destination, dumping the bag in a nearby laundry cart.

Having fixed a gold-coloured badge to his breast that bore the name 'Renard', and the hotel logo, he headed up the stairway to the penthouse floor where he was permitted access to the suite by other hotel staff, on the pretext of bearing an important message for one of the occupants. Once inside the suite, the senior staff member who directed 'Renard' to the meeting room did not see the blow that incapacitated him and he crumpled silently to a heap on the floor. Gogol dragged the man into a nearby cupboard and closed the door. There was no need to eliminate this individual who was just doing his job after all, and he felt no need to restrain the man, as this mission would be completed in a matter of minutes.

Grabbing a silver tray to preserve the element of surprise for as long as possible, he placed an envelope with a man's name, and no other information, on the tray and raising it to shoulder height, knocked purposefully on the meeting room door. As Gogol entered the room, he immediately observed a large oval shaped mahogany table with six men and an attractive blonde woman seated around it, all obviously engaged in a business meeting. Although he knew who they were, he had never personally met any of the group before, nor them, he.

All seven of the occupants instinctively turned their heads to the door as Gogol entered, at which point in English, but with a heavily inflected French accent, he spoke;

"Pardon me for the interruption lady and gentlemen, but I have an important message."

Having no idea what Max Simpson actually looked like, Gogol walked over to the blonde female, the only person in the room he could confirm was not Simpson, and lowering the tray presented her with the envelope. Natalie Caldwell picked up the envelope and having read the name of the addressee, she laughed lightly, and offering the envelope to the impeccably dressed man two seats to her right said, "Max, it's for you."

Gogol, acutely aware that all in the room were Bectel's top executives, and complicit in project *Chrysalis*, immediately snatched his pistol from under his tunic and unleashed six head shots which dully thudded out of the silenced weapon, instantly killing all the occupants of the room except the chairman Max Simpson who, shocked and surprised and still holding the envelope, sat motionless at the head of the table in the sights of the assassin's weapon.

"Gogol!" he hissed in horror, in the sudden realisation that this man was his company's most secretive and deadly asset. "What the hell do you think you are doing?"

Gently closing the door to the meeting room and pressing the device that electrically closed the curtains of the room, Gogol stood just eight feet from his quarry.

"The one thing in my life," Gogol began with raw indignation in his voice, "that cannot be compromised, is the love that I have for my Country. You knew that."

"I never married and never had children, so that I would never have to make the choice between those that I love, and my country. You knew that also."

"I accepted the offer Bectel had made me, and I have done your bidding for nineteen years because it did not compromise my love of my country, and now I learn that in less than forty days' time you are going to unleash project *Chrysalis* upon the world." "An event," he continued, "the magnitude of which humanity has never before witnessed, and which will bring about the destruction of most of the world, including my homeland and everyone in it."

"Why was this information withheld from me?" he demanded, raising his voice.

Max Simpson opened his mouth to speak but Gogol continued regardless.

"And what is worse is that if this catastrophe is permitted to come about," he said emotionally, the pitch of his voice rising towards a rare display of anger, "I will have been complicit in the destruction of my own people!"

"That, Mr Simpson," he said with abject determination in his eyes and a rapid resumption of his ice cool emotional demeanour, "is something I cannot, and will not permit to happen. I want to know it all, right now. I want to hear it from you, the where and the when, starting with Harrison Becker's current location."

Realising the gravity of the situation he now found himself in, for the next few moments Max Simpson complied, corroborating what Gogol had already uncovered on *Funtime* and confirming that the countdown was indeed underway and could not be stopped. Simpson proposed the only course of action he could imagine that would dissuade the expert assassin from ending his life.

"Let me call Mr Becker personally," he offered in desperation. "I am sure that we will be able to modify the plan in a manner that you find palatable."

Gogol raised his weapon, pointing it directly at Max Simpson's head and hissed through clenched teeth, "I've seen the projection and I know what happens. I think not, Mr Simpson."

As he squeezed the trigger of his pistol, two 9mm bullets crashed through Max Simpson's skull within millimetres of each other, knocking him backwards off his chair, instantly ending his life.

Gogol wiped down the silver tray, clearing it of any identifiable marks and, grabbing the envelope off the table, left the suite returning to his own room several floors below, where he gathered his belongings and after briefly logging on to *Funtime* and exchanging some information, he disappeared into the night.

Having reverted to the persona of Bernard Deauchamp, in case he encountered a police random stop, Gogol sped through the darkness in his rented car heading for the principality of Monaco where, as Simpson had just confirmed, Harrison Becker's yacht was currently berthed, undergoing restocking of supplies and some minor mechanical procedures.

Passing through the Mont Blanc tunnel into Italy, Gogol headed for Turin then turned southwards to join the Italian Riviera west of Genoa, before following the coastline southwest to Monaco, stopping only to eat and refuel.

Chapter 28

It was 3.15am on the morning of 12 February and in the windless African darkness, Marvin 'Stogie' Harris, by far the most senior of the four B2 Pilots stationed at Camp Lemonnier American airbase in Djibouti, Africa, stood in quiet contemplation with his colleagues.

The four men had just been briefed on their top-secret mission to deliver a low yield nuclear device to a 'not yet specified' target, somewhere in central Africa. Stogie and his number two, Calvin 'Riptide' Bottomley, stood alongside their backup B2 crew at the edge of the briefing hangar, the three men waiting impatiently whilst 'Stogie' finished his trademark 'potentially last cigar', a superstition that he observed before every flight and which had earned him his pilot nickname, almost twenty-eight years previously.

"So!" 'Riptide' said, running his free hand through his thick black hair. "What do you make of it skip?"

"This is the real deal my friend!" 'Stogie' replied, vectoring a puff of smoke carefully away from his colleagues. "The fact that they have not yet specified our target, and backed us up with a second crew means that this is so hush hush and secret, that they really can't afford for this mission to fail."

"And what is your take on the coordination with three other assets?" 'Riptide' added.

"Can't say," 'Stogie' replied. "Other than it adds to the intrigue, doesn't it?"

"All I know is we will proceed generally towards our target and get the precise coordinates once we are in the air. After that, all we have to do is launch our weapon exactly when instructed and get the hell out of the way so that 'Sinbad' and 'Postman'," 'Stogie' was referring to their colleagues in the backup crew, "can launch their weapon a minute later." "Then it's the worst bit, the waiting!" With that, 'Stogie' sucked the life out of the last of his cigar and jammed the remnants into a sand bucket, positioned just outside the door. Both crews then made their way out into the darkness and to their aircraft which were fuelled, armed and ready to depart.

Ten minutes later 'Stogie' and 'Riptide' in their B2 Stealth Bomber, their mission clock now running, left the runway to climb into the darkness to their cruising altitude, with 'Sinbad' and 'Postman' following closely just off their starboard wing.

Having reached forty-five thousand feet, the aircraft levelled out at which point 'Riptide' received the long-anticipated targeting coordinates on the aircraft computer, crosschecking with 'Postman' that he had the same information.

Both crews were instructed to proceed west over central Africa and then southwards in an anti-clockwise circular pattern in order that they could approach their target from the west. At a range from target of 50 miles, 'Stogie' would receive instructions to launch his weapon, with the backup strike weapon being launched by 'Sinbad's' aircraft exactly 60 seconds later.

"Wow 'Stogie', check it out!" exclaimed 'Riptide', who had now extrapolated his targeting information. "It looks like we are about to strike a huge pyramid next to a hospital complex in the north DRC. I wonder what that is all about?"

"I don't know son," said 'Stogie'. "That kind of brain power is way above our pay grade but one thing you can be sure of is that, considering the secrecy surrounding this mission, there will be a bloody good reason for it."

Unknown to the two airmen, similar conversations were being had by sub mariners on station in the Pacific, and both US and British aircraft carrier-based pilots in different parts of the world. Operation *Colourfield* had begun and was now being coordinated by US Air Force personnel out of CIA headquarters in Langley, Virginia.

Four individual weapons platforms were soon about to launch their specially adapted weapons which, through careful calculation and coordination, were all intended to strike their targets at precisely 5.30am GMT, and thousands of miles away in London and Virginia, two rooms full of men and women waited anxiously on the outcome of that attack.

Chapter 29

The time was now 5.00am GMT in the COBRA briefing room on 12 February, the morning of the coordinated operation, and Langley had already announced the launch of USS Virginia's cruise missiles, which would strike the *White Horse* pyramid at Kiritimati in precisely 30 minutes time.

The remaining weapons, all being delivered by aircraft, were already airborne and would be launched at a range of 50 miles from their individual targets, striking the west face of each pyramid. Once launched from their respective aircraft, the remaining missiles would have a flight time of just seven and a half minutes until they delivered their nuclear payload.

As the clock reached 5.22am GMT, Langley confirmed to all three flights that their target was 'go' and to prepare for launch. Thirty seconds later all three flights confirmed a primary weapon launch, as did the backup aircraft, launching their secondary weapons precisely one minute later.

As the missile telemetry began broadcasting, Langley was now confidently predicting that all four primary strike weapons would impact their targets within ten seconds of each other. As the clock counted down, silence reigned over both committee rooms being broken only by the commentary from the mission commander at Langley control centre, reporting the progress of the weapons and counting down the seconds until first impact.

At precisely 5.30am, Langley control reported that the Kiritimati pyramid had been destroyed. Cheers broke out from both meeting rooms and by the time the uproar had been quelled, Langley had confirmed the destruction of the remaining three pyramids, and that data from 'real time' satellite reconnaissance, relating to the radioactive footprint from each site confirmed that the Ammonium Perchlorate propellant had been neutralised, rendering all four pyramids inert.

The primary weapons having completed their function, Langley initiated the abort instructions of the secondary's which, now redundant, were all harmlessly destroyed in mid-flight.

Just when it had begun to subside the cheering, supplemented by rapturous applause broke out again, with much hugging and back slapping going on, at either end of the video link.

Through cooperation, ingenuity and meticulous planning, operation *Colourfield* had been a resounding success.

Grant Wilson sat quietly in his seat, and for the first time in over a week permitted himself to crack a smile of satisfaction. He looked across the table at his MI6 colleague Marcella Houston who unashamedly gave him a giant double thumbs up sign, then mimicked to him, by lifting a semi clenched hand to her face, that she could do with a drink.

At 6.00am Connie Chapelton called the video meeting to order and when all was silent, she began to speak, reading the script from the more palatable of the two possible scenario's she had prepared for this moment.

"Ladies and gentlemen," she began, waiting for the satellite delay to kick in stateside and quell the celebrations that were still ongoing. Silence restored, all eyes were now focussed on her.

She began by clearing her throat.

"Thank you all for some splendid work over the last week or so, in identifying and neutralising the threat to world stability posed by Bectel. We have ably demonstrated that by cooperation and consultation, by asking the right questions of the right people, the human species can accomplish the seemingly impossible. We collectively, have today, made history in taking definitive and decisive action against a threat that was set to exterminate almost 63 percent of the human population, and destroy society as we know it. The debrief of this incident in the weeks to come will detail the actions of each and every one of you, and the part that you have played in averting this crisis."

"From my perspective, and I speak on behalf of the entirety of the British government, I would like to thank and congratulate CIA Director Alfonso DeSouza, his staff and all of the US joint chiefs, for the perspective they have brought to this incident. And not forgetting all you experts in your individual disciplines too, for the technical knowledge and background you were able to deliver in support of this operation." "Not least" she continued, "the US Navy personnel who were able to modify and transport the tactical nuclear warheads timeously and deliver them with precision, in order to achieve our objective with minimal loss of life." This generated a round of applause from the UK cabinet briefing room directed at the 'cousins' who permitted themselves a smile of satisfaction.

"Similarly," she resumed, "I would also like to pay tribute to all on the UK side for their efforts in bringing this crisis to a satisfactory conclusion, not least the key actions of MI6," as she looked across the table, locking eyes with Marcella Houston who was beaming with pride. "Additionally," she went on, "and I know he will castigate me for doing this, but I must give special mention to Commodore Grant Wilson of the British Royal Navy, a brilliant strategist and tactician without who's foresight and analysis, we would have been chasing shadows to the ends of the Earth." She motioned for Grant to stand up, which he reluctantly did, to rapturous applause from both the room and the other side of the video screen.

The PM continued, "Follow up teams have been dispatched to

each of the four sites to assess and contain, and when their work is completed, we will reconvene for a comprehensive debrief. Both the Chinese and Russian governments have been made aware that the threat is now neutralised, and I plan to meet with each in the next day or two to fully debrief them on the incident. In the meantime, I now release you all from the confinement imposed by this committee, and would remind you all that what you have witnessed this morning and over the last few days is, and will remain, top-secret."

"Alfonso?" she said, inviting the CIA director to pitch in with his comments. Alfonso DeSouza stood up and addressed the meeting;

"Madam Prime Minister, members of the UK government, leaders of the UK armed forces, scientists and technicians, and of course the 'Joint Chiefs' and all of my colleagues stateside."

"The President of the United States of America has been following this crisis closely and I have just, moments ago, briefed him on the success of the operation on which he asked me, on behalf of all humanity, to pass on his heart felt congratulations to all involved."

"As we have previously discussed, this incident will not appear in the headlines anytime soon and although they are still partially standing, the destruction of the west face of the pyramids will be reported by the world's media to be caused by a catastrophic design flaw."

There followed a short round of congratulatory goodbyes, whereupon Connie Chapelton formally closed the meeting.

"I'm off for a hot bath and a long sleep," she said linking her arms with Grant and Marcella, "and then I'm going to have to debrief the leaders of the other UK political parties and then, 'whoop de doo' she said sarcastically, it's the Chinese and the

Russians."

At that, the three friends and colleagues went their separate ways, the PM to her home at number 10, Marcella to her Chelsea flat and cats in London and Wilson headed for his hotel.

Chapter 30

It was around 8.30am the following morning, the 12th February when Gogol arrived in Monaco, completely unaware of the actions the British and American governments had just undertaken against Bectel.

Gogol's luxury limousine merged inconspicuously into the light traffic carrying the numerous occupants of the principality to their various weekend leisure pursuits, on what was otherwise a bright Saturday morning in the pleasant Mediterranean sunshine.

About ten minutes later, having changed in a nearby gas station, Gogol arrived at Port Hercule Marina, a haven for the boats of the rich and famous. Although Gogol had never actually visited the company ship before, the 96-metre long Bectel Yacht, with its helicopter on deck, was not difficult to locate and wearing a set of maintenance coveralls and carrying a small tool bag, he made his way to the vessel which bore the name *'Quelle Surprise'*, which was moored up and apparently unoccupied.

Gogol made his way across the passerelle and onto the yacht, unaware that his every move was being watched by Harrison Becker, who was in a special room in the bowels of the, 500 million dollar vessel. As he entered the superstructure on the main deck, Gogol stealthily closed the privacy glass doors behind him, his sole intention to locate and eliminate the main threat to his beloved homeland; Harrison Becker.

Suddenly, a soft voice rang out from the internal PA system speakers, seamlessly blended into the ceiling of every room of the interior of the vessel. "Good morning, Mr Hazan," the voice announced, calm and composed. "I have been expecting you."

"I would very much like to speak with you face to face Mr Hazan. I have some information that you may find to your advantage. Please follow the central staircase down two levels and proceed towards the bow of the vessel until you see a silver coloured, steel door. When you get there, press the green button to gain access to the chamber beyond. I will await you there." With utter disregard for his own safety, Gogol followed the instructions of the voice which had uttered his birth name, a name that he had not heard spoken aloud for over nineteen years, and as he approached the silver door, he drew his pistol.

Pressing the green button as instructed he entered the room, finding himself in a luxurious chamber approximately 8 metres wide by 15 metres long. The room resembled a conference room with the entire wall at the opposite end from the door dominated by a giant television screen, incorporating many small screens within, in 'picture within picture' mode. The many screens displayed various views of the interior and exterior of the vessel.

Although the two had never actually met, Gogol recognised Harrison Becker from an old picture in Time magazine, the man himself sitting like a statesman behind his large desk. Although Gogol could not see the lower half of Beckers body, he observed that the man's poise was relaxed with his elbows on the desk and his hands, devoid of any kind of weapon, clasped together with what appeared to be a glass of orange juice near to his left elbow.

Gogol, suspicious at the ease with which he could enter with his pistol drawn and end this man's, life looked again at the makeup of the room. His instincts told him something about the chamber wasn't right, but he could not quite put his finger on what that was. Although the ships engines were not running there was nevertheless a low hum that his ears could just barely discern.

Harrison Becker motioned for Gogol to sit in a green leather armchair, slightly to the left of the door but still a good six metres or so from his desk. Gogol, at Becker's invitation seated himself, reaffirming the grip on his pistol and pointed it directly towards Harrison Becker.

Becker calmly began. "Please do not feel threatened Mr Hazan. If I intended any harm to you, it would have happened by now. Please help yourself to some water," indicating a small table to Gogol's right which contained bottled water and a crystal glass.

Then suddenly it dawned on him. Gogol realised that, apart from the television screens at the far end of the room and some tables positioned somewhat randomly, the walls of the chamber were completely unadorned. But why, he pondered?

Becker continued. "First of all, I need to tell you that I will not permit you to harm me Mr Hazan, not until you have heard what I have to say."

"You will find your pistol quite ineffective in this room. I am sure a man of your calibre will have noticed by now my apparent vulnerability, which like many things you may have experienced recently, is not quite what it seems to be. Although the pistol you are holding is composite plastic, the ammunition it uses is not, and I am quite safe from any projectile your hi-tech weaponry could fire at me. The low hum, your ears have no doubt become accustomed to by now, is an induction motor built into the walls of this room and which generates a very powerful electromagnetic field. The electromagnetic field is such that it can detect and divert the path of a bullet, and even at this short range your deadly aim would have no effect, but I am rather hoping that when you find out what I have to say to you, it will not come to that."

Becker's comments made sense to Gogol who had experience of the innovative technology available to the company, and although unconcerned for his own safety and trusting his instincts, he deliberately placed his pistol on the table and, pouring a glass of water, sat back to listen to what Harrison Becker had to say.

"We, Mr Hazan," Becker began, "are approaching the climax of an elaborate plan, a plan many years in the making, conceived by me and only made possible by the considerable power and wealth I have at my fingertips. I am talking about Project Chrysalis." Having previously consulted the *Funtime* website, Gogol was familiar with the codename and what it represented.

"Like you Mr Hazan, I cannot contemplate the destruction of my homeland and have done all within my power to prevent such a catastrophe from ever taking place."

"For you, Israel is your homeland and is what you have dedicated your entire lifetime to protecting. I dare say that in coming here, you are ready to exchange your own life for that of your people. A very noble and admirable sentiment Mr Hazan, and not completely dissimilar to my own personal feelings."

"Yes, I too wish to preserve my homeland, although for me the word homeland represents a little bit more than the borders of a small, if albeit much loved, country."

"As you are no doubt aware I was born in Austria, but since then I have travelled the world extensively Mr Hazan, a journey that has been for me, enlightening, fortuitous and profitable." "I'm talking about the world Mr Hazan, the whole world, my home and it is under threat of destruction and, like you, I do not intend to stand idly by while others destroy it."

"You have seen the simulations on the *Funtime* website, I assume, Mr Hazan?"

Becker's question caught Gogol completely by surprise. He shifted uneasily in his seat and reaching, for the water glass, took a sip before returning the glass to the table, his hand held there still, steady and only inches from his pistol.

From this position Gogol could grab the weapon and loosen two accurate headshots in under a second, and in doing so would test the claimed effectiveness of Becker's bullet deflecting electromagnetic field. But he did not. Instead, he waited and with a poker face, kept his hand on the glass trying to show no indication of the conflicting thoughts flashing through his mind.

How did Becker know about *Funtime?* Did he know about the note in the truck?

Gogol had assumed that the informant, whom he had been conversing with on *Funtime,* had been MI6 or CIA. Did Becker know that less than 12 hours ago, of his own volition, Gogol had assassinated Bectel's entire executive team?

Until now Gogol had thought that the information on Becker's true intentions had come from British or American intelligence and that *Funtime* was operated by them. But now?

It was apparent that this now was obviously not the case, and for the first time in a long time, Gogol found himself 'wrongfooted'.

Becker was watching the man closely, and seemingly aware of the confusion playing in Gogol's mind, he spoke the answers to Gogol's unspoken questions, those answers coming in quick succession.

"It was I who arranged the note in your truck Mr Hazan, and it was I also, with whom you have been corresponding and who passed the information that you now possess, to you via the *Funtime* website. I knew that if you had been compromised you would follow default protocols and contact Stanley Harding, and I knew that following what I had to show you, you would locate and eliminate him, which is why I instructed Max Simpson to convene a meeting of my top executives, in order that they would all be in one place when you came calling."

"I fully anticipated what your reaction would be Mr Hazan, and I knew also following that reaction you would come looking for me."

"And here we are!"

Confident in his approach, Becker continued. "The truth is Mr Hazan, I am not afraid of death. If I cannot employ my considerable resources and my talents to defend my homeland then, what is the point of living? I would deserve to die."

"So let me make this one request of you Mr Hazan."

"Please listen to what I have to say to you, following which I will deactivate my magnetic field rendering myself vulnerable to your skills."

"If you still wish to kill me, then it will be simplicity itself for you to do so."

"What do you say, Mr Hazan?"

Unused to being mentally outmanoeuvred in this way, Gogol was still trying to process what he was being told. It didn't make sense! Why would Becker want his entire executive team eliminated? To break the 'stale mate' Gogol responded calmly.

"Ok Mr Becker, it's a deal. You have my word, and now my undivided attention."

Becker went on to explain the real and immanent threat to the Earth from global warming, that he had recognised years earlier, and of his attempts with the Chinese and Russians to take corrective action in order to head off the looming global disaster and of the subsequent negative reaction he had received upon offering his help.

"To be honest Mr Hazan, after my assistance had been rejected by the Chinese, I had no option but to take matters into my own hands."

"The projection I unveiled to you on the *Funtime* website of how *Chrysalis* would affect the Earth within two years, is a highly accurate depiction of what would happen, if the pyramids had been permitted to ignite and fulfil their purpose."

Becker was now speaking in the past tense however Gogol, at this point, did not pick up on it.

He went on to add, "However, without action from the worlds superpowers the same situation will come about in less than 50 years from now, so as I am sure you can appreciate, doing nothing was not an option for me."

"That is why I conceived and executed project *Chrysalis*. It was an open and very credible threat, designed to bring about a worldwide calamity and spur the world's most influential nations into an unprecedented era of cooperation and immediate action, in order to avert a global catastrophe."

"As you now know, the event was designed to auto ignite on 20th March, however if I so desired, I could have at any time set the whole thing in motion with the press of a button." Becker indicated a small glass prism on the right of his desk, which was actually a retina scanner constructed of unbreakable sapphire glass, which when activated would immediately initiate project *Chrysalis*.

"Of course, the decision makers in London and Virginia will have anticipated this eventuality, which would have further motivated them on to address the challenges I had set them, increasing the reliance they have on each other."

"And it has been successful Mr Hazan. In the last week or so, the world's most influential nations have taken notice. They have had secret meetings and have cooperated to address the threat, forming strategies to identify and neutralise the fire power of my pyramids, all with the goal of preventing *Chrysalis* from coming to fruition."

"And now Mr Hazan, through that cleverly orchestrated

cooperation of the world's most influential nations, I can reveal to you that at 5.30am GMT this very morning, project *Chrysalis* has been neutralised, completing phase one of my plan to redeem the world."

"Now, I would fully expect that there will be a worldwide manhunt for those responsible, however it will not take the world long to ascertain just who those people are, and thanks to you Mr Hazan, they are all now dead."

"But those people were your executive team. People you trusted!" Gogol exclaimed.

"Trust is just an emotional response to certain aspects of human behaviour, Mr Hazan, and I learned a long time ago that in business, emotions can be a handicap. They were all expendable Mr Hazan. Necessary tools for me to achieve my goal."

"As for you Mr Hazan. Your part in this was to consolidate the reality my threat would pose. You neither knew or had an inkling on what I was planning, and loyally carried out orders issued to you through the chain of command. You are blameless in this whole affair and, for what it's worth, you can take consolation that instead of assisting in the destruction of your homeland, in a roundabout way your actions have directly contributed to its long-term stability."

As he said this Becker, calculating the susceptibility of Uri Hazans emotion state, pressed a button on his desk deactivating the magnetic field. The dull humming sound now having stopped, Gogol sat for a few seconds in thoughtful contemplation and then reaching for his pistol, he re-holstered it within his coveralls.

"So! I'm convinced. What now Mr Becker?" Gogol enquired.

"Now Mr Hazan, the world is listening, and it is time for phase two of project *Chrysalis*. I want you to immediately cease all 'enforcement' operations on behalf of Bectel Inc.

"Are you firing me, Mr Becker?" Gogol asked uncertainly.

"On the contrary Mr Hazan. Your loyalty and your integrity are beyond reproach. You have carried out my vicarious instructions dispassionately and with ruthless efficiency. You are intelligent, logical and possess skills that no one else in this organisation could possibly acquire." "No, Mr Hazan," Becker reiterated, "you are not being fired." "There is no evidence to indicate the services carried out on behalf of Bectel were attributable to you, and any witnesses with sufficient information to the contrary are now dead."

"Therefore, I am promoting you Mr Hazan. I want you to take the *Quelle Surprise* to Bectel HQ, in Papua New Guinea, and I want you to be my deputy CEO and run my company whilst my attention is focussed on phase two of my project."

Gogol was taken aback. "But Mr Becker. You do know that I came here with the intention of killing you?"

"Yes, I know," Becker replied, "but I was confident that when you grasped the bigger picture, I would be able to dissuade you."

"While I'm gone, I want you to kick start the research into the Trans Warp Propulsion System that we had previously been working on before this whole situation began, and when we do make a breakthrough Mr Hazan, you can be sure that your beloved nation will be included in the roll out discussions at an early stage."

"My lawyers have been ordered to open instructions at midday today that will ensure a smooth transition of power, effectively making you my deputy CEO, and putting you at the helm and in full control of Bectel in my absence."

"May I suggest that you begin by setting up meetings ASAP and avail yourself to the department heads, who will do what they can to assist you. They are all good people Mr Hazan and innocent of any involvement in project *Chrysalis*."

"All of the information that you will require to do this, is contained in my files at HQ in Mendi," he said, following up with, "and you will be able to access any information requiring a password by entering your old service number."

"And one more thing Mr Hazan," Becker said. "As of today, I do not want to hear the name Gogol mentioned again. Gogol ceases to exist as of this moment. Use your given name as it is time for you to come out of the shadows."

Totally taken aback by all that he had just learned Hazan, visibly perplexed asked the question.

"So, Mr Becker. Where do we go from here?"

"Now I want you to take me to the airport Mr Hazan. I'm off to London where I will hopefully be meeting with an officer of the British Royal Navy, who just happens to be one of the smartest men on the planet."

"I suspect the superpowers and others, who shunned my advice several years ago, will now be ready to listen to me and with this man's endorsement, I intend to complete phase two of my plan and lead the efforts to combat global warming, the *true* long-range threat to our respective homelands."

At Nice, Cote Dazur Airport fifty minutes later, Uri Hazan stood on the tarmac with the man who only hours earlier he had targeted for termination.

"Your private jet is fuelled and ready for boarding sir," an impeccably dressed female flight attendant said, greeting Becker on his arrival and directing him up the staircase of the aircraft.

"Thank you, Miss Marshall."

"Keep in touch Uri and good luck," Becker said.

As Harrison Becker turned to board his jet, Hazan called out to him. "That was a big risk you took in switching off that machine Mr Becker, if indeed it does what you claim it does."

"Yes, it was Uri. A carefully calculated risk, and to gain your comprehension and cooperation, was one that was worth taking," adding, "also yes in answer to your query, the machine does indeed do what I claimed it does."

"Be mindful of that Uri, as the path we are now intending to follow," referring to the development of the TWPS, "will not please everyone and you may need it in the future."

Chapter 31

It was 7.30am by the time Wilson arrived at the lobby of the Chesterfield hotel, which was waking up to the day ahead, and as he made his way to the elevator a voice caught his attention.

"Commodore Wilson," the duty receptionist called over to him.

"Yes," he replied.

"A message for you sir," she said, offering an envelope to Wilson, adding, "hand delivered by courier this morning."

"Thank you." said Wilson taking the message. "Can you send room service up to my suite please with some breakfast for me? I would like Porridge made with water and salt." This was an absolute must for Wilson, keeping alive the Scottish method of preparation of this most stable of foods, into which he would pour double cream, an indulgence he inherited from his father. "And a full English breakfast, with coffee and toasted brown bread. Also please send up some yoghurt and a selection of fresh fruits."

"Yes sir," the receptionist replied, immediately summoning service staff from the far side of the hotel lobby.

Once inside his room, Wilson put his attaché case and the message on a side table and, muttering to himself something about priorities, stripped out of his uniform and made directly for the shower. After scrubbing the grime from his body, he stood under the hot water for a full ten minutes, rejuvenating his jangled senses.

Donning a luxurious robe, adorned with the hotel motif, he

returned to the lounge of his suite and in the second precisely calculated event of that day, room service arrived 'on cue' with his breakfast cart. The waiter entered the room where Grant permitted him to uncover his porridge and pour his coffee, before dismissing him with a thank you and a small gratuity.

Grant decided that whatever the envelope contained, it could wait until he had eaten as he figured that whatever the message was, it would probably require him to do something to the detriment of his much anticipated breakfast. Munching on the food, Grant sat watching the morning news channels to try and catch up with what else was going on in the world, paying particular attention to a breaking news story regarding a mass shooting at a hotel in Switzerland.

A short time later having eaten, he pushed the breakfast cart aside and filling his coffee cup from a silver pot and adding a modicum of cream, he stretched out on the sofa opening the envelope which was addressed to 'Commodore Wilson'.

Inside was a single sheet of card which read:

Congratulations Commodore Wilson

London City Airport, runway 09

Tail Number N-5023

Wheels up 1230hrs

Come alone, we need to talk

HB

Wilson immediately picked up the room telephone and called reception. The desk clerk answered the call promptly with a welcoming and friendly tone.

"Good morning, Hotel reception, Andrea speaking. How may I help you?"

Grant spoke directly, with no inclination for any pleasantries. "This is Commodore Wilson in suite 259. Was it yourself Andrea who gave me a white envelope containing a message this morning?"

"Yes sir, it was," Andrea replied.

"You said it was hand delivered by courier?"

"Yes sir, that is correct."

"At what time?" Wilson asked.

"About fifteen minutes after I came on duty this morning sir. That would have been about 6.45am."

"Did you see the courier?" Wilson again asked.

"Yes sir," the clerk replied, "but he had a motorcycle helmet on so I could not see his face clearly. Is there a problem sir?"

"No. There's no problem," Wilson replied. "Thank you, Andrea," adding, "wait. Do you have a hotel limousine?"

"Yes sir," Andrea replied. "We have four," she offered enthusiastically, trying to make up for whatever it was that had seemingly put the hotel guest on edge.

"Have one meet me out front at 11.45am promptly," he requested.

"No problem, sir, consider it done," she said decisively."

"Thank you, Andrea." Wilson concluded, hanging up the phone.

Wilson pondered the situation for a moment and then scribbled his thoughts on a piece of hotel notepaper, 'just in case' he thought, and, addressing it to Marcella Houston, he put it in his attaché case for safekeeping, along with the message from Becker, in the event his instincts were wrong.

Donning the few clean items of casual clothing he had left in his travel bag, which were jeans, a striped short sleeved shirt, a heavy sweater and his favourite red 'Kicker' boots, Wilson made his way to the lobby of the hotel where his limousine driver was waiting.

Once seated in the vehicle he instructed the driver to proceed to London City Airport, a short twenty minute or so, ride away.

At the airport check in desk, Wilson enquired about N-5023 and its 12.30pm departure. The desk operative delicately lifted a telephone and spoke softly to someone on the other end of the call.

"That's Mr Wilson just arrived to check onto your flight," she said politely.

Moments later an impeccably dressed female flight attendant, wearing a tan trouser suit uniform, appeared from a back office and in a polite English accent addressed Wilson;

"Good afternoon, Mr Wilson. My name is Alicia. Your aircraft is fuelled and ready for departure. If you would kindly follow me, please," she said, leading him to a departure gate which led to the runway area.

Once 'airside', Alicia led her guest to a waiting airport vehicle, which had a flashing yellow light on the roof, a requirement for all airside vehicles at UK Airports. There was a driver in the vehicle and its engine was running. Opening the rear door and motioning for him to enter, Alicia then climbed in to the front passenger seat herself. Without speaking, the driver drove to the runway perimeter where a white and gold coloured Bombardier Global 7500 jet, tail number N-5023, Harrison Becker's private aircraft and one of a fleet of six belonging to Bectel, was waiting.

The 70 million dollar aircraft's twin engines were running and the ground engineer was standing adjacent to the cockpit, attached to the aircraft by an umbilical cord, making arrangements with the pilot for an imminent departure.

Alicia led Wilson from the car, up the steps and onto the aircraft and motioned him to a seat in the plush cabin, which looked more like a cocktail lounge than an aircraft. Operating the controls which secured the door, Alicia made her way into the main cabin as the plane started to taxi out to runway number nine.

"Your host will join you shortly after take-off," Alicia informed Wilson, with a beaming smile and, ensuring he was strapped into his seat, she made her way through a door to the rear of the aircraft. Within minutes the jet was climbing high over central London and as it levelled out and adopted its pre-planned course, the pilot spoke through the intercom.

"Good afternoon, Commodore Wilson," he began in a polite and efficient tone.

"Our flight path this afternoon will take us south and east over Belgium and Luxembourg. It is not our intention to land in Luxembourg but merely complete a loop over the country before returning to London, over French air space. Our flight time will be approximately two hours, twenty minutes and the weather will be fine for the entire trip, with no turbulent air forecast."

"Miss Marshall will be offering you some refreshments in a few moments and your host will join you shortly. I hope that you enjoy your flight and, in accordance with CAA regulations, I can advise it is now safe for you to remove your seatbelt."

As the pilot signed off, the cockpit door opened and a man in a tailored grey business suit made his way into the main cabin and introduced himself with an air of confidence.

"Commodore Wilson," he began. "I have been so looking forward to meeting you in person. Harrison Becker," he announced, extending his hand in the customary business greeting.

"I have heard so much about you," he said, firmly shaking Wilson's hand and seating himself opposite.

"Can I get you anything?" he asked, pressing a small button on the arm of his luxury chair as he sat. Almost immediately, Alicia appeared from the rear of the aircraft and made her way towards the two men. Becker addressed her formally, but with respectful affection.

"Miss Marshal. Commodore Wilson will have a Macallan 18 year old Scotch whisky, with just the smallest drop of water," subtly indicating that he had researched his guests background extensively.

"Thank you, Mr Becker, but no thank you," Wilson replied. "It's a bit early in the day for me."

"Some champagne then?" Becker enquired.

Wilson conceded to the champagne with a slight nod of his head.

"Splendid!" Becker exclaimed. "Miss Marshall, would you bring me a bottle of chilled 'Moet et Chandon', and kindly prepare a light lunch for two please."

As Alicia Marshall disappeared into the rear of the aircraft, as an icebreaker Becker started the conversation;

"As I'm sure you are aware Commodore Wilson, my company is not short of funds, but I just so like the taste of *Moet*," he remarked, using the universally accepted abbreviation for the brand, "as compared to the other more expensive, less aromatic champagne's available." "To me the drinking of such expensive vintages can be a little...", he hesitated looking for the appropriate word, "pretentious, don't you think?" "Chosen by people who are perhaps more interested in impressing others, and who are not really what they seem to be," he concluded, casting a cryptic look towards Wilson, on whom the sentiment was not lost.

A short time later, Alicia entered the cabin pushing a cart containing the champagne in a silver ice bucket, a lunch of lobsters, various other seafoods, a light green salad, and an accompaniment of various breads and fruits. Wilson candidly noted that the cart also contained a pot of freshly brewed coffee and a small jug of fresh cream, a detail he observed that was unlikely to be a coincidence.

Pouring a glass of champagne for each, Alicia left the room sporting her beautiful smile and reminded both men that should they require anything they need only call her. She closed the rear cabin door and left the two 'adversaries' alone.

"Mr Becker," Wilson began. "I assume you know what I have been doing for the past week?" he remarked, involuntary raising his left eyebrow in a manner that suggested, was it all possible that Becker did not know about Wilson's role in the operation to thwart Bectel's plan? "And of all the people in the UK, you asked *me* here to meet you," putting a lot of emphasis on the word, me. "May I ask why?"

"Simple old man," Becker replied. "To congratulate you on a first-class job well done, very well done indeed."

Mindful that the top-secret plan to destroy the pyramid structures had concluded only a few hours earlier, Becker's exchange with Wilson exuded the confidence of a man who knew everything.

"But Mr Becker, I am having difficulty understanding," Wilson said.

"I, and others," he said, still being guarded about how much he was prepared to reveal to Becker regarding his activities of the previous few days, "have collaborated in an operation which has destroyed more than six years of your organisations work, and laid waste to tens of billions of dollars of your company's funds."

"Also, and I have to be honest Mr Becker and say that, due to the activities of your organisation, you are now one of the world's most wanted men. The CIA have issued a capture or kill order on you!"

"As for me," Wilson went on. "My curiosity has obviously gotten the better of me."

"My career and my freedom are at stake in my just being here, so pardon my scepticism Mr Becker," Wilson said, and nodding in the direction of his glass added, "but this is likely to be the most expensive champagne I have ever tasted in my life."

Becker had time to strike a knowing smile before Wilson continued.

"Having received your note, I admit your initials got my attention and I was curious, thinking your invitation to a flight would be a way for you and I to meet virtually, on a video screen and in an environment where you could control the conversation, but I never thought I would be meeting you in person."

"I mean, how did you even know what I have been involved in, and when and where I would be, in order you could send me that note?" he said, sounding uncharacteristically bemused.

"Commodore Wilson," Becker began, "or may I call you Grant?"

"Yes. Grant works for me," Wilson replied.

"In which case, please call me Harrison," Becker replied cordially.

"Firstly," Becker began, clearing his throat and motioning for Wilson to eat.

"As for the tens of billions of dollars of Bectel funds. You may consider that money well spent, and what you might well describe as..." he paused for thought, "investment capital."

"As for knowing all about you! You are no doubt aware Grant, that my organisation has probably the best intelligence service in the world and without exaggeration, my people could give the combined intelligence resources of MI6 and the CIA a good 'run for their money'."

"I have, of course, been aware of the meetings taking place between yourselves," Becker was referring to British Intelligence and the CIA, "as regards your perceived threat to global stability. And I am further aware that initial assessments of the raw intelligence data indicated that I was developing a Trans Warp Propulsion System for the Chinese or the Russians." "Good Gracious," he blustered. "I'm not surprised you all came to that initial conclusion, as it was my resources that dropped *that* trail of breadcrumbs for your intelligence services to follow."

"Incidentally," he added, "Trans Warp Propulsion for space travel is theoretically possible and closer than you may think, but we will save that conversation for another time."

Going on Becker said, "I have been following your career for some time Grant, and when the COBRA meeting was convened to address the situation which I had created," his use of the past tense alerting Wilson to the extent of Becker's intelligence stream, "then it was only logical that you, the author the of the UK Naval Cyber Warfare programme for the 21st century, would be summoned from your base in Scotland to attend."

"It was not such a leap from there for my people to confirm your involvement in that meeting Grant, and that information pleased me as I believe quite honestly, none of the others would have been able to figure it out in time which would have resulted in, if I may use the vulgar expression, my 'bluff' being called."

Wilson interrupted. "Are you saying that you spent billions of dollars on a scheme so 'out there' that virtually no one could figure it out, and then looked to others to do just that, and sabotage your own operation?"

Becker reply was simple and to the point. "Yes," he said.

"But why?" Grant replied, munching on a piece of celery he had selected while Becker had been talking.

"No. Don't answer that, Harrison," Wilson added, rapidly regaining his composure.

As Grant's lateral thinking brain engaged, he said; "Let me see just how much of this I've got right?"

Becker motioned for his young adversary to continue and, sitting back in his chair picking at a lobster claw, he listened intently.

Wilson began chronologically and followed, what was to him, a logical narrative.

"It is well known that you are a steadfast environmentalist and opponent of the global warming phenomenon, and have been so for many years, long before everyone else jumped on the bandwagon. In fact, I seem to remember seeing you on television many years ago when I was a boy, meeting with Attenborough, discussing the plight of the Polar bears." Wilson was making reference to the globally renowned natural historian, Sir David Attenborough.

"Through your intelligence department, you probably figured out that the Chinese, closely followed by the Russians no doubt, with their rapid expansion plans, were the main contributors to global warming and decided that with your vast financial resources you were in a position to do something about it."

"Using your position, you probably approached them to reduce emissions offering them some sort of incentive to do so." Becker's silently nodded, indicated to Wilson that he was on the right track.

"Trans Warp Propulsion! You offered them Trans Warp Propulsion, and all of its benefits, if they would curb their emissions," concluding, "and they turned you down!"

Becker continued eating and nodding, as Wilson went on;

"They turned you down," he repeated, "probably not something you are accustomed to, and so you found yourself backed into a corner."

"Hence you conceived operation *Chrysalis?*" he asked hesitantly.

Becker nodded in agreement, his eyes now sparkling with delight.

"And your pyramids, which we now know were actually gigantic rocket motors that when ignited, were designed to speed up the Earth's rotation, cooling the whole planet and heralding a new ice age, halting the onset of global warming in its tracks. But killing almost three quarters of humanity in the process."

Not wanting to interrupt Wilson in full flow, and wiping seafood sauce from his lips with a white linen napkin, Becker answered simply, "Yes, please go on."

"And, the Northern Hemisphere being more land than water, would suffer most, effectively punishing the two biggest nations responsible, China and Russia. But also taking out the rest of Eastern and Western Europe, Scandinavia, Canada, North America and Australia in the process."

"Collateral damage unfortunately, none of whom are blameless I hasten to add," Becker retorted.

"And this was planned for when all the pyramids were completed and primed, and the Northern Hemisphere would be just coming out of winter so would be at its coolest, maximising the effect of your actions." "Logically, to me," Wilson proffered, "the Spring Equinox, 20th March 2022."

Clear of the process of eating for the moment, Becker clapped his hands gently together in genuine applause, and again wiped his lips clean with his napkin.

"At 9.37am GMT, to be precise," Wilson added.

"You surpass yourself Commodore Wilson," Becker replied, reverting temporarily to a formal address to underscore how impressed he was at his guests' conclusions.

"Of course," Becker said, "the final chance for the world leaders to redeem themselves was at the COP 26 climate conference, in your native Glasgow last November, but as usual the leaders would huff and puff and procrastinate, predictably making a few hollow promises that would make the newspaper headlines but in truth would turn out to be hopelessly inadequate."

Continuing with his narrative, Wilson went on;

"By my reckoning the spring equinox was the ideal time to ignite your weapons, but anytime would have had a similar devastating effect to the world. Am I correct in assuming you had an override facility?"

"You are indeed," Becker said. "On board my yacht, where I tend to spend most of my time these days." He then added, "The event would have auto ignited on 20th March at 0937 by default, had you not stopped it, but I could have initiated the process from anywhere on the planet should I wished to have done so, a failsafe so to speak, and necessary to lend credence and urgency to the threat the world was facing. And just for your information, I was rather banking on not having to use the override but believe me Grant, and between you and me, if it came to it, I would have," he concluded in a sombre tone.

"Without definitive action, the Earth is doomed anyway," Becker continued ruefully. "Project *Chrysalis* was merely intended to speed up the process."

"But Harrison," Wilson exclaimed. "You would have been responsible for the mass murder of over five billion human beings!"

"Even though it is now not going to happen," he added, "the world is still going to want your head for contemplating it in the first place, and coming so close."

To which Becker added solemnly.

"And that, my dear fellow, brings us to why I have invited you here."

Chapter 32

As the aircraft headed south east, just crossing into Belgian airspace, Becker asked inquisitively, "I am curious to know Grant. How did you figure it out?"

Wilson, satisfied that Harrison Becker was indeed well informed on the UK governments activities, could now see nothing detrimental in sharing this information with the man who conceived operation *Chrysalis*, a project for which he was mainly responsible for scuttling, therefore he began;

"The first thing for me was the location of the pyramids," he said. "Positioned equidistant around the globe and almost on the equator where their function, whatever it was to be, would be likely to have maximum impact."

"Then, each pyramid having a west facing side. I was already suspicious that the orientation was relevant, and when supplemented by the finding of Benjamin Ngoy's paper blueprints after his plane came down, showing the weaker west face, it confirmed my suspicions that it was designed to implode at a predetermined time."

"Afterwards came the satellite footage of the intense fire at the Tumeli residence, which burned with such intensity that our satellites reported it as a missile launch putting NATO on high alert. I had a hunch then, and following reports of the intensity of the blaze in which nearly all victims' bodies had been vapourised, I revisited the autopsy report and ordered a chemical analysis of the remains found at the bottom of the well. The answer came back as Ammonium Perchlorate, which I knew to be the fuel used in the twin SRB's on the space shuttle programme."

"Having already figured out the pyramid codenames referred to the four horsemen of the apocalypse, I realised that the pyramids were actually four gigantic rocket engines, designed to bring about Armageddon."

"Due to the western orientation of the weakened side, I reasoned that when ignited, the vectoring of the energy contained within the pyramids was designed to speed up the rotation of the Earth, shortening the Solar day and plunging the whole planet into a new ice age within about two years."

"And the solution?" Becker enquired. "I am so interested to hear about that."

"There were a number of options," Wilson added, "but neutralising the propellant seemed the least harmful to me, so it went to a discussion and the committee thankfully decided 'neutralisation' was the best option."

"Did *you* formulate the chemistry to neutralize the propellant?" Becker enquired with interest.

"No," Wilson replied emphatically. "I knew what was required, but chemical engineering is outwith my field of expertise, so I called on the services of a 23 year old acquaintance of mine, who as it happens is a genius in the field of nuclear chemistry."

"Having previously calculated the likely quantity of propellant in each pyramid, I gave her some numbers and she worked out the nature and mass of a small thermonuclear device that would be sufficient to render that propellant inert."

He continued, "Although it was I who provided the parameters required for the operation to be effective, it was a real team effort and the bulk of the credit goes to the Americans who actually made it happen. They provided the devices, the weapons expertise, the logistics and coordinated the simultaneous strike operation and well," Wilson said, "you know the rest."

"Thank you for that Grant. Perhaps I need to have this genius nuclear chemist of yours come work for me," he said, winking at Wilson.

"So here we are!" Becker continued, drawing together the threads of their clandestine gathering, and rapidly approaching the climax of his long set plans.

"In essence Grant, project *Chrysalis* was a very expensive bluffing exercise, designed to give the arrogant misguided leaders of the world's superpowers an exercise in humility." "*Chrysalis* was ultimately intended to fail," he revealed.

"The whole operation was an elaborate plan, conceived in order to unite the world's leaders, spurring them into action that would cause them to cooperate to address the *real threat* to humanity," putting much emphasis on the words *real threat*, "That threat being global warming, and the irreparable damage that the phenomenon is doing to the environment."

"And you found yourself to be an essential, if albeit unwitting, part of that plan Grant."

"Believe it or not, I was counting on you, and others like you, to divine a solution under which the world leaders would unite, setting aside their petty differences and personal agendas to save our planet, thereby proving that with the right motivation, anything is possible."

"But like I said Grant, make no mistake. If you had not stopped *Chrysalis*, it would have auto ignited at the Spring Equinox, and all that you had forecast would have come to pass."

There was a silent pause which seemed like an eternity to Wilson until Becker, reverting to a lighter tone announced; "But thankfully it didn't happen. Those that could, did what they should have done twenty years ago. They united and formed the solution to a threat, saving humanity and enabling our way of life to continue with what will now be a few crucial, but necessary changes. However I seriously doubt if any of the world's population will be reading about this in tomorrow's newspapers," he said, knowing full well that the British and American governments would keep this incident buried in their secret file archives for at least the next one hundred years.

"Those others however," he used the word *others* with disdain in his voice, meaning primarily the Chinese, "that were responsible for the rapid escalation of global warming in the first place will now realise what a near miss they have had and, with the correct leadership, they will be only too happy to collaborate with each other and deliver 'new and innovative solutions' to save our planet."

"Solutions, I hasten to add, that will be environmentally friendly but also conducive to the continued and sustainable proliferation of the human race. And I wish to be the one who provides that leadership," he said, as he prepared to reveal to Wilson the ultimate goal of project *Chrysalis*.

"Which, is where you come in, Commodore Wilson," again reverting to a formal address of Wilson to signify that he was coming to the crux of his plan.

"Me? "Grant remarked in surprise, taking a large drink of iced water and sitting up in his chair. "Why me?"

"Why not?" Becker exclaimed. "As the hero of the hour, I am sure that your voice will carry some weight in explaining my side of the story to the NATO leadership." He then added, by way of a plea of mitigation, "Notwithstanding the default position that *Chrysalis* would have auto ignited at the Spring Equinox had you not succeeded, then I personally," he said touching his right hand to his heart, "have done little that could attract any serious criticism."

"Ok, I will concede that there have been a few dead drug dealers along the way, which no one will mourn."

"And a couple of Civil Servants that had met with an early demise, but to be honest Grant the UK and American governments, along with the Chinese, The Russians, The Israelis and whoever else, carry out that sort of 'wet work', in the name of their own interests every single day."

"Yes Grant. *Chrysalis* was conceived and financed by Bectel, and created with the sole purpose of uniting a hesitant world against global warming, for which I unashamedly accept full responsibility."

"It is a sad fact however that, in making it happen, my executive team appear to have, rather unfortunately, misinterpreted my wishes and overstepped their role somewhat. Consequently, it is they who will posthumously carry the blame for the innocent casualties in this whole affair."

As Becker uttered the word posthumously, Grants mind flashed back to the morning news report, of the killing of several, as yet unidentified individuals, in a Swiss hotel the previous evening.

"The Swiss hotel incident!" Grant said, leaping to a conclusion. "They were your people?"

"Yes," Becker replied, showing no emotion at the loss whatsoever. Becker went on, "What appears to have been a 'rogue element' in my organisation have operated beyond their brief in their incorrect interpretation of my wishes. They are now no longer of use to me and have been suitably dealt with."

"You see Grant," Becker said dispassionately, his memory briefly drifting back to his childhood pet dog 'Jake', "I learned a very hard lesson from my father a long time ago that in business, to succeed in your goal, you need to focus and be prepared to dispense with assets that have outlived their usefulness, before they become a liability."

Chapter 33

Harrison Becker's jet landed at London City Airport at 3.20pm and a few moments later Becker, standing adjacent to the aircraft door, shook hands with his guest and bidding him farewell remarked, "Thank you for meeting with me today, Grant. I do sincerely hope you will be able to convey my side of the story to your superiors," finishing with, "I'll be in touch."

Miss Marshall assisted Wilson disembark from the aircraft into a waiting vehicle before reboarding the plane, which taxied to the main runway and took off again, heading for an unknown destination.

As Wilson entered the airport terminal he switched on his mobile phone and called his friend Marcella Houston, who was enjoying some well deserved rest at her home. Marcella, awakening from a deep sleep, answered the call groggily, somewhat angry at being prematurely roused from her slumber.

"Grant!" she said, somewhat perplexed at the interruption. "What the fuck?" adding rhetorically, "Don't you ever fucking sleep?" It was clear that the MI6 chief was in no mood for small talk.

"Does your phone have a secure line?" Grant enquired.

"I'm the MI6 Chief of Secret Intelligence," she snapped, referring to her official job title to add emphasis to her foul mood. "All of my fucking phones have secure fucking lines," she added, as sarcastically as her current state of mind would allow, hoping her tone conveyed the enormity of her displeasure at the untimely awakening.

"Well, you're going to need one of them!" "Go to channel, Delta 6."

Grant heard the tones in his receiver ring out as Marcella dialled the code for channel Delta 6 on her handset. He did likewise, and immediately heard an automated message stating 'super encryption channel 6 active', following which he heard Marcella's voice, somewhat softened in the realisation that encryption protocols meant that there would be a sound and legitimate reason for the intrusion.

"I'm sorry Grant. I guess I'm just a little bit tired and cranky," she said, with what could have been the slightest trace of remorse on her voice. "I am certain you are aware, but you do know I've been awake for over thirty-six hours trying to *SAVE THE WORLD*?" elevating her voice at the last three words, effectively emphasising that encryption protocols or not, she had still not fully forgiven him for waking her.

Grant was about to begin with; '*Guess who I have just met?*', but realising the folly in this course of action with his friend and colleague, at that particular juncture, he simply went with, "Can I trust you to be discrete?"

"Of course," she said, her senses honing in on what was an unusual question for her friend to ask her.

"I've just had a face to face, with Harrison Becker!"

There was a stunned silence at the other end of the phone while Marcella processed the information.

"*Thee* Harrison Becker?" she said. "Are you shitting me Grant?" was all she could further manage to break the silence.

"The one and only," he replied.

"But there is a capture or kill order out on him and unless he's dead, or lying beside you in handcuffs, you could be in big trouble."

"I know," said Wilson. "But having spoken with him, I think you are going to have to convince the 'cousins' to rescind the order."

"And why on earth would I want to do that?" she exclaimed in total disbelief.

"The answer to that one is just too hot, even for an encrypted phone call. You still in London?"

"Yes. I'm at my flat in Chelsea," she replied.

Wilson answered decisively. "I'm in Central London myself. I'm getting a cab and will be with you, in about twenty-five minutes. Put some coffee on," he said, adding, "you're going to need it." And with that Wilson cleared the call and exiting the airport, hailed a cab.

The traffic in London was a little busier than expected and Wilson arrived at Marcella's Chelsea flat thirty minutes later. Marcella answered the door in blue jeans and a baggy sweater with her hair in a towel, having just stepped out of the shower.

She amiably invited Wilson in to her luxuriously appointed flat, and made her way through to her very large dining kitchen which, through a five-panel retractable glass wall, overlooked a pristine and beautifully landscaped private garden at the rear of her property. Away from work Marcella lived a paradoxical existence. She loved a well tended garden, but detested gardening. Her generous salary and Yoki, her Japanese gardener, were the answer to that paradox.

Grant sat at the breakfast bar and Marcella, pouring a large coffee with cream for him, and a black coffee for herself, sat opposite.

"I'm sorry about the potty mouth," she said in genuine apology, knowing that Grant knew her well and of course would forgive her. "I get a little cranky when I'm tired."

"Don't I know it," said Grant with a wry smile.

They chinked their coffee mugs together in a gesture of mutual friendship and forgiveness and then Marcella, frustration all vented, calmly said, "Ok Grant. Tell me all about it."

Grant went on to relay to his friend all that had happened since his arrival at his hotel that morning, from being presented with the message, right up until when he disembarked Becker's plane and entered the airport concourse.

"Fucking hell!" was all that Marcella could manage, seemingly forgetful about her recent apology for her language, but this time the curses were not directed at Wilson.

"We have to tell Connie about this ASAP."

"Well, if you don't mind, you can make that call," Wilson proclaimed, "because I am not waking her." "I've heard enough cursing and swearing for one day as it is," He said, pulling a mock look of fear on his sharp, handsome features.

Marcella, still with a mouthful of coffee, screwed up her nose at Wilson and putting her coffee mug down on the surface, she reached for her mobile phone. Pressing only two buttons she was directed to MI6 headquarters and was connected directly to her colleague and deputy Chief of Secret Intelligence, Robert C. Jenkins.

"Bobby," she said as soon as her deputy answered the phone.

Immediately recognising her voice Jenkins replied, "Yeh boss, what's up? Shouldn't you be asleep or something?" he added, unwittingly risking an earful of abuse from his department head.

"No shit, Sherlock," she snapped in reply, making sarcastic reference to her colleague's detective abilities by comparing him to Sir Arthur Conan Doyle's great literary crime solving sleuth. Reining herself in from a full blown audible assault, she said instead;

"Get the COBRA incident room up and running ASAP."

"I want our legal people in on this one, and please find and wake the PM. Tell her this is Priority 1 intelligence, and she needs to hear it directly from me. Tell her Grant Wilson is with me and we are heading over to her place now."

"Also get me everything you have on Harrison Becker, and get a hold of Interpol. I want everything we can get on that mass shooting at the Ritz Carlton hotel in Switzerland yesterday."

"Factoring in a stop at 'number10', I'll be in Whitehall in about 90 Minutes." "And Bobby," she added.

"Yes boss," he replied.

"Minimal staff please, 'need to know' basis."

"You got it boss," he said, as she terminated the call.

Connie Chapelton sat on the sofa of her private quarters, above the formal rooms of no 10 Downing Street, and listened to the brief being verbally delivered by her intelligence chief, with supplementary questions being answered by Wilson.

Unusually, even though the trio were in private, the air was remarkably free of expletives, a known and much discussed trademark of the Prime Minister's seemingly uncontrollable frustration.

"So, let me summarise," said the Prime Minister, having heard

234

what the duo had to say and with an unquestionable note of astonishment in her voice.

"Becker has put the entire world in danger, spending billions of dollars on a threat that he was willing to carry out without compulsion, on the justification that it was inevitable anyway."

"But he wants us to ignore the events of the last week, and convince the world leaders to believe that his actions were indeed, just a mega expensive motivational exercise?"

"And, as if that wasn't a big enough ask, he is claiming that several of his people have misinterpreted his instructions and gone 'rogue', killing or executing several civilians to keep his plans on track."

"And now he wants us to just forget all that because, by way of atonement, he wants to lead a group of world leaders through a process that will prevent the global warming phenomenon reaching a tipping point, thereby saving humankind."

"Have I got all that right?"

Both Wilson and Houston looked at each other and turning to Connie Chapelton, in perfect unison, both nodded their heads together and replied, "Yes."

"Well, that's all right then!" she said, disparagement practically dripping from her mouth. The respite was over and Connie Chapelton's sarcasm was beginning to ramp up. "For a minute there I thought I was fucking dreaming."

"Between us and the cousins, we have just spent tens of millions of pounds and dollars, of our respective taxpayers hard earned money, on finding a solution to the global threat that Becker created, and now that it's all over he wants us to just forget it and shake hands?"

"Connie," Wilson cut in, trying to prevent the Prime Minister's tone from unnecessarily rising any higher in pitch.

"Becker's angle on this is that, we were only successful in our solution because there was an imminent and credible threat to our way of life, and collectively we felt compelled to act on it, out of our sense of self preservation, if nothing else. His position regarding global warming remains the same. His issue is that we," Wilson was referring to the world superpowers, "don't *or won't*, recognise the gravity of the situation, and in true political fashion we are prepared to 'kick the can' some way down the street," using the metaphor to suggest that today's politicians, out of arrogance or ignorance, are prepared to leave the Global Warming phenomenon for somebody else to deal with.

Thirty Minutes later a somewhat placated Prime Minister Chapelton, MI6 Chief Houston and Commodore Wilson shared a car back to the COBRA briefing room in Whitehall, London, where they would soon engage in another video conference with select members of the Central Intelligence Agency and none, other than the President of the United States himself.

Chapter 34

It was now late May of 2022, and an unsuspecting world had moved on following the Bectel incident and the events surrounding the response to neutralise project *Chrysalis,* were already assigned to the confidential files of the British and American secret services.

In the affluent village of Hambleden in the county of Buckinghamshire in rural England, retired teacher Ruby Cameron was pottering around in her garden, feeding and pruning her collection of roses, in anticipation of the beauty and the explosion of colour their blooming would soon bring. It was a pleasantly warm spring morning and the only sounds that could be heard in Ruby's garden were the buzzing of insects and the clip of her pruning shears.

The hour was approaching 11.00am and Ruby, who had been at her labours for most of the morning, decided it was time for that most civilised of pastimes, morning tea, and went into her kitchen to prepare her favourite beverage just as her old friend Judith Gordon arrived at the garden gate.

Ten minutes later the ladies were sitting at a wicker garden table, absorbing the sights and sounds of springtime in England, enjoying some shortbread biscuits and sipping tea from antique China teacups, once owned by Ruby's Grandmother.

The women had been friends since they were children and had always enjoyed each other's company. In their working lives Ruby had been an English teacher and Judith a Civil Servant, however both had been retired for just over ten years now. Although they were both widows, they were independent women, financially comfortable and now able to enjoy the fruits of their respective careers, which in Ruby's case was one in which she had never experienced even one day of sickness absence.

The two friends, like most of the world's population, some of whom were doing the exact same thing at the exact same time, were blissfully unaware of how close the Earth had recently come to disaster that, which among a great many other things, would have meant the end of their favourite pastime which was sitting together and enjoying the sights, sounds and smells of the garden.

Thoroughly enjoying this particular blend of tea leaves, sipping delicately from her cup and addressing herself out loud, Ruby remarked;

"I've said it before and I'll say it again Ruby. You have a special knack for making the perfect, cup of tea." To which, as if reading pre scripted lines from a play, her friend Judith replied;

"And just how did you achieve that, Ruby?"

Answering with a smile of satisfaction on her face, her China saucer held at chest level and raising her cup in the air, Ruby replied;

"Tea, milk and just a spot of honey, all mixed together in perfect *equilibrium,*" she giggled.

Epilogue

It was 2.00pm on a cool September day in 2022, at the conference centre in Ankara, Turkey, where the newly elected chairman of the *United Nations Against Carbon Emissions* council (*UNACE*), stood ready at the rostrum to announce how innovation and worldwide cooperation were the key to arresting global degeneration, and be the platform from which humankind could combat the effects of the global warming phenomenon.

Introducing the man, the speaker concluded his introduction with the phrase;

"Ladies and gentlemen, may I now introduce you to the new Chairman of *UNACE*, the CEO of Bectel Incorporated, Mr Harrison Becker."

During the secret conferences that had taken place between the UK and American governments, immediately following operation *Colourfield,* both nations had unanimously decided to accept Becker's explanation of the events leading up to and during the crisis as 'plausible', concluding that the urgency and innovation which led to the success of operation *Colourfield* should be seen as an ardent demonstration of the kind of cooperation that could be achieved, when the motivation to do so was strong enough.

Having agreed a course of punitive action and financial compensation to be paid by Bectel, for all those directly affected by the crisis, Harrison Becker's 'capture or kill' order was rescinded, and he was thereafter free to enter both the UK and United States.

Becker would shortly thereafter present proposals for the

formation of *UNACE*, a select but powerful group, who would possess both the financial and political clout necessary to achieve a programme of industrial reforms and carbon neutral processes, that would eventually halt the production of harmful carbon emissions from being expelled into the Earth's atmosphere. It was universally agreed that this innovative range of measures, if implemented immediately, would bring harmful emission to an abrupt halt, and reverse the Earth's decline as soon as 2027.

Becker was as good as his word, and would go on to draw on the huge financial resources of Bectel to achieve this end. As well as becoming the duly elected leader of *UNACE*, Harrison Becker did indeed go on to receive the Nobel Peace Prize in relation to the Hospital complex at Kisangani in the DRC and for its contribution to peace and stability in the area. The facility went on to be completed, utilising conventional power generation methods, despite the incident at the nearby Kisangani 'Play Station' which, like the other similar structures around the globe, was blamed on a catastrophic design flaw.

His time being totally consumed by leading the fight against global warming, Harrison Becker announced that, in his absence, he had appointed a new deputy to run his company. The individual he chose was someone that he literally, trusted with his life. An intelligent man, of whom Becker was heard to say;

"One who would motivate Bectel's new executive team of experts in new directions, and spearhead the drive into keeping all aspects of Bectel's international business interests alive and thriving." That man being none other than Mr Uri Hazan.

Under Hazan's leadership, Bectel went on to accelerate their space exploration programme, committing huge financial resources to the development of a Trans Warp Propulsion System which, with the recruitment of new talent, was now several steps closer to reality.

Speaking at a scientific conference in the Autumn of 2023, Bectel's new 'Director of Interstellar Development' would conclude her brief confirming the company's commitment to humanity, and making a solemn declaration to the people of the world. She ended her speech with a bold statement;

"...and when fully developed, the Trans Warp Propulsion System will be shared by all, to facilitate space travel in support of our ultimate goal, which is the sustainable proliferation of the human race." It would soon be reported by the world's media, following the conference, that Bectel's new Director of Interstellar Development, was none other than Professor Ekaja Chopra, OBE.

The operation to identify and neutralise project *Chrysalis* was indeed confined to the national security archives and would be kept secret for the next one hundred years. The devastation which occurred at each of the pyramid sites was explained to the world as a catastrophic design flaw in the structures, all of which would be demolished when the minimal radiation occurrences at the sites had completely dissipated.

Antonio Varas's government did achieve a landslide victory in the Ecuadorian elections early in 2019 and went on to accomplish an unprecedented further three terms in office. Backed by Bectel's capital investment proposal, the Varas government did indeed go on to complete their education reform programme, which achieved worldwide acclaim and was very much the key to the *Nueva Herencia* government's enduring popularity. Antonio's relationship with his personal secretary Sebastian remained a closely guarded secret, up to and after their relationship came to a natural end.

Sir Durnian Cruickshanks went on to retire as Admiral of the Royal Navy with full honours in the Autumn of 2023 following which he was made a Lord of the Realm, taking a seat in the British 'House of Lords', bringing his significant experience to bear in shaping the policies and the economic direction the UK would choose to follow in the forthcoming years. Sadly, Lord Cruickshanks died of lung cancer in early 2024, attributed to his heavy smoking in the early days of his naval career.

Following the Bectel incident, and largely attributable to the endorsement of the British Prime Minister, Commodore Grant Wilson would undergo further accelerated promotion within the British Royal Navy. This began immediately following operation *Colourfield,* with a brief spell as Rear Admiral of the Fleet, followed by a Vice Admiral role, before being promoted to Admiral of the UK Royal Navy in the Autumn of 2023, taking over directly from his friend and mentor, Lord Durnian Cruickshanks.

Being age 35 at the time of his appointment Wilson gained yet another career accolade, becoming the youngest ever officer to reach the rank of Admiral in the modern Royal Navy's history.

Although he was based in Portsmouth, and following a 'Knighthood' bestowed on him by the newly crowned King Charles III, Sir Grant Wilson made a point of retaining his family home in Scotland, to which he would return at every possible opportunity, duties permitting.

Following the sad and untimely death of the incumbent US Vice President in early 2023, the former Director of the CIA, Alfonso DeSouza, was nominated as Vice President, directly